The Noble War

Chandni Khawaja

ISBN: 0692025154
ISBN-13: 978-0692025154

To my parents, who inspired me. Goaded me, even.

CONTENTS

ACKNOWLEDGMENTS

Over a span of three years, this book was born. Like a fresh sapling, it was nurtured and corrected and watered daily and corrected again. During this journey, I received prodigious help from Emily Bengels, a teacher, a mentor, and a friend. For her assistance, optimism, and humor along my winding writing road, I am greatly indebted.

"War does not determine who is right—only who is left."

Bertrand Russell

I

TUNNELS

As Chell proceeded down the long hallway, her footsteps echoed loudly through the cavernous corridor. Tall, thin torches flickered from the crumbling stone walls and cast long shadows on the earthen floor. Their wavering glow failed to adequately light the gloomy space.

"How far does this tunnel go?" the girl wondered.

Ahead, she could see nothing but a dark, dusty hole. Gradually, Chell could hear mice scurry away in the shadows. She went further down the endless path and heard the sound of water dripping from the ceiling.

"Water. There might be an end to this tunnel," she muttered.

Chell quickened her pace. A foul air wafted through the halls and she wanted to leave as soon as possible. She grabbed a torch off the wall to better light her way. As she walked briskly, the dripping became louder and fell in a rhythmic pattern that sounded like the ticking of clocks. Out in front, there was a faint, unfaltering light, but it was too cold to be that of a torch; the light was an odd blue instead of an orange flame. Chell narrowed her eyes in puzzlement and slowed her pace. The light became brighter as she inched closer, and through the warm mist in the tunnel, Chell could see a figure.

Sitting on a large, decorated block of what appeared to be obsidian was a middle-aged woman with jet black hair. Her frosty blue eyes pierced Chell's soul and sent shivers down her spine. When she saw Chell, the woman smiled as if she had been waiting a long time for this moment. Chell shifted her focus to the woman's palm. A glowing blue orb that was composed of some sort of eerie liquid hovered above her hand. Behind the woman hung a sturdy, ornately carved door that arched at the top.

Chell stopped and gazed at her surroundings. A tiny, barred skylight was cut into the ceiling, but no light shone down from it. A small waterfall had broken through the decrepit walls, created by an underground spring or well. The water splashed down and soaked much of the floor below, but the mysterious woman's long, midnight-blue robe was spared from the liquid; the black hem seemed to levitate above it. Fat, brown mice emerged from the shadows and ran to and fro. They disregarded the woman, the water, and the girl. The mysterious woman didn't seem to notice. Her eyes were determinedly fixed on the torch-bearing figure in front of her. She opened her mouth to speak. Chell waited expectantly for an introduction and an explanation, but the woman was not interested in small talk.

"Do you know what lies behind this door?" she asked mystically.

Chell didn't respond. The aged figure scared her but also intrigued her. A small voice in the back of her mind urged her to run, but to where? There was nowhere to go.

"I said, do you know what lies behind this door?" the woman asked in the same oracular tone.

Snapping out of her contemplation, Chell shook her head. "No. Should I know?"

The odd woman's smile grew larger. "You will know, child, when you are ready for the information."

"I'm ready now," the girl replied, becoming more and more desperate as time wore on. *She looked over her shoulder at the misty darkness of the hallway. Chell could feel a lurking terror watching her in the shadows, waiting for her next move.*

The sorceress threw her head back and cackled. The sound echoed frighteningly down the dark corridor.

"How can you be ready?" she said.

Chell shifted her weight to one leg and crossed her arms. This woman was really starting to irritate her.

"It's not like I have any other choice," she replied with irritation. "There's nothing else in that stupid hallway. What else am I supposed to do?"

The woman nodded towards the hallway behind Chell. *"You can go back. You can wander forever in that dark, dank corridor. You can travel forever with fear and apprehension of what lurks in the shadows. Or,"* she motioned to the door, *"you can be enlightened. You can see what will come out of all that uncertainty and doubt. You can see the possible future of your world."*

Chell stared blankly at the woman. "Are you telling me I could see the future?"

"The near future, to be exact," the sorceress replied, nodding.

"Or, I can continue living like I am right now. Not knowing."

"Correct. Your choice, Chell."

At the mention of the girl's name, the curious orb glowed brighter and turned a darker shade of sapphire. It scared Chell, but at the same time captivated her in a way that she couldn't explain. It called to her, yearned for her. Entranced, she could barely feel herself moving closer towards it. As the woman calmly looked on,

Chell reached out her hand to gently touch the orb. When her fingertips made contact, a sharp, burning pain seared through Chell's arm and an invisible force propelled her backwards onto the wet ground. She cursed loudly as she grasped her arm but saw that no visible damage had been done.

"Not yet, child. In time, you too shall wield this, but that day has yet to come."

"What is that thing?" Chell shouted as she picked herself up.

"This is power, Chell. Power in its purest form," the woman sighed as she gazed at the orb with desire.

"Well, I have no intentions of using that thing. None whatsoever."

"It is not your choice whether or not you will obtain it. It is your destiny."

"Then I'll change my destiny!"

"Oh, come now, child. Do not be foolish. You are fully aware that you cannot do that. Besides, how can you change what you do not know?" The woman swept her hand in front of her and motioned to the door. "Step through the doorway and you will see what shall come to pass."

Chell shook her head in bewilderment, walked forward, and placed her hand on the brass doorknob. She took a breath and flung the door open. Before her, there was total darkness. Both fear and guarded excitement gripped her heart and her hands began to sweat as she imagined the visions that awaited her.

"Remember," the woman warned. Her voice seemed to come from another dimension, though she was right behind Chell. "I only said that this is the 'possible' future."

Chell became hopeful. "So the real future will be better, right? It's not gonna be pitch black?"

The sorceress laughed again, but this time her laughter was dark and ominous. "Quite the contrary."

With that, she grabbed Chell's shoulders and shoved her through the door. The door slammed shut and a giant lock clicked from within. Panicked, Chell lunged at the door with her full weight and tried to open it, letting out frantic screams as she did. Behind her, a fiery light slowly grew, illuminating the dark space. Her back became warmer and warmer until she felt like she was standing next to a bonfire. Shrieks and yells filled the air and echoed all around her. Seized by fear, Chell turned around to face the fate of the world.

Fires raged through a once-bustling metropolis. All around, looming skyscrapers crumbled into the flames below, releasing giant clouds of ash and dust. Fire hydrants and water lines ruptured from the heat and sent tall columns of boiling water into the air. People scattered wildly in all directions amid the chaos. Children wailed as their mothers clung to them while others limped, crawled, and dragged themselves across the street in a desperate attempt to escape. The flames grew steadily higher and the ground began to shake. The people tried to get as far away from the road as possible.

"They're getting closer! They've come for us! They're here!" a young woman cried in dismay.

Who or what was here, Chell didn't know, but she had a bad feeling that it was something foul. She helplessly directed her gaze down the street and her eyes grew wide in terror as the source of the destruction unveiled itself. From the flames rolled out a machine unlike anything Chell had encountered before. It was an immense tank with the most sinister array of weaponry she had ever seen. Gun ports stuck out from all sides and pointed directly at the citizens on the sidewalk. Its head was crowned by a wreath of barbed wire. Its massive wheels rumbled forward and flattened cars and debris. The celadon unit appeared to be impenetrable.

More followed after the master tank. Three, four, five machines made their way down the street in a V-formation. People on the side backed away but none tried to flee; the fear that had gripped them had turned their resolve into jelly. Chell pivoted to follow the path of the tanks, which finally halted in the middle of the avenue. Nothing moved except for the flames. The tanks stood as if dormant, great hulking pieces of metal and might. The wails of the dying and of sirens in the distance were muffled as a fearful anticipation rose from the crowd. Chell waited, too, as the sound of her own beating heart pulsed painfully in her ears.

Suddenly, the tanks awakened by some inward command and fired upon the crowd. A massive flight ensued but most did not get far. Sound reentered the world and renewed screams filled the air, followed by the sound of bodies hitting hot pavement. Chell watched as they fell, chests and stomachs blown out by shells the size of stones. Blood filled the streets as they drained out of their lifeless owners. Merely a specter and unable to be seen or touched, Chell trembled and walked forward. The faces of men, women, and children stared up at her with cold eyes while icy fingers brushed against her ankles. Some corpses were missing limbs and even heads, so powerful were the guns on the tank.

She slowly looked up and saw the avenue was empty, save the advancing tanks. Chell hoped that no one would be foolish enough to get in the way of the instrument of death. A cry sounded from across the street told her that she would soon be proven wrong. A young child, no older than three, ran into the road.

"MA! MOMMY!" he screamed as he held his fat little arms outwards. His mother lay injured in the street.

"No, darling, go back! Go back to the sidewalk! Don't come to Mommy! DON'T COME TO MOMMY!" the woman wailed.

Too late she realized that nothing could stop the crying boy, so she tried to reach him. Fear surged through Chell's mind as the young mother limped towards the child. When she met up with him, the head machine slowly turned towards them like a villain in a bad dream. The pair froze in silent terror as the weapon rumbled closer. Inside the killing machine, gears turned and whirred. The main gun lowered and remained at eye-level with the mother.

In a last desperate attempt to save the family, the woman scooped the toddler into her arms and tried to run. However, the pressure on her twisted ankle sent intense pain shooting up her body and she collapsed with her child still in her arms. The machine moved over the couple almost lazily. The young woman cradled her son close to her as the arm prepared to strike. Then, with the speed of a lightning bolt, it fired.

Chell's eyes bolted open and she sat up fast. Her heart raced and her breath seemed ready to escape from her chest. She was sweating, but her skin was as cold as death. As she tried to steady her breath, she glanced at the digital clock on her nightstand. It was only two o'clock in the morning. Outside, rain pattered against the windowpane.

"It was just a dream," Chell reassured herself silently. "It was all just a dream."

But as she settled back into bed, closed her eyes, and tried to sleep, the vision of mother and child consumed in explosive flames replayed over and over in her mind.

II

DAYBREAK

At eight o'clock, Chell's alarm clock blared. Silencing it, she sat up in her bed and rubbed her eyes. She ran her hand through her tangled hair before trudging to the bathroom with a groan. Chell peered at herself in the mirror and made a face. Her hair possessed none of its usual sleekness and dark circles ringed her eyes. Chell took a quick shower and the icy water quickly banished her tiredness. After blow-drying her streaming hair, she drew it back and fastened it with a clip. It gleamed like onyx once again. The girl went to her closet and pulled out a simple black sweatshirt and a pair of dark jeans. Her wardrobe was limited as it was, but she didn't have the heart to dress in colors after her chilling dream. She took one long, final look at herself, grabbed her bag, and proceeded quickly down the stairs.

Chell walked into her small kitchen and saw her father reading the newspaper with marked boredom. Her little brother Jack spooned cereal into his mouth while her mother washed the dishes and hummed. When she heard Chell come down the stairs, she stopped.

"Morning, honey. Off to school so soon?" she asked, hugging her daughter while trying not to get soap all over the countertop.

"Big exam today, so I'm going to study with the group," Chell replied distractedly. Although there was some truth to her story, there was a weightier explanation for her early flight.

Chell's mother smiled as she released her daughter. Chell skirted around towards her father, who was still scanning the paper for something interesting. Finding nothing, he grunted slightly and put it down. Finally acknowledging his daughter's presence, he smiled at her. Chell walked over and planted a small kiss on the top of her father's head.

"Mornin'," he said as his daughter peered at the newspaper that was lying askew on the breakfast table.

"Nothing new here, I see. As usual," Chell replied, tapping two fingers on the newspaper's cover.

"No, nothing. It's been talking about the same old thing for years; I doubt anything new is going to happen today."

"Hmm. Shouldn't you be getting to work now, Dad?"

"Work?"

"You know. That thing you go to, doing...whatever it is that you do. What do you even do, may I--"

"Goodness, you're right! I nearly forgot!" her father interjected. He rose abruptly from the breakfast table and strode over to the coat hook. He agitatedly put his windbreaker on but tried to hide his nervousness with a laugh. He affectionately patted Jack on the back as he got his second arm through his sleeve. Going to his daughter, he hugged her tightly and planted a kiss on her head before moving to his wife.

"Have a good day at work, honey," she said quietly after they broke from their embrace.

"I always do," he chuckled with a wink. Chell's mother merely pursed her lips.

With that, he exited the kitchen, grabbed the car keys from the foyer, and left. Chell shook her head as she heard the car pull away.

"Are all fathers this strange?" she asked her mother in quiet puzzlement.

"Yes. Some more than others, though. I'll admit that," Chell's mother said with a frown as she went back to her dishes.

Chell noted the strangeness in her mother's tone but said nothing. Instead, she walked over to the other side of the table and ruffled her little brother's hair.

"Hey, kiddo. Shouldn't you be off to school soon?" the girl asked.

"Nah, I'm gonna skip it today," Jack said in reply.

From the sink, Chell's mother said, "That's what *you* think."

Jack smiled. "I'll be leaving in fifteen minutes or so.

Chell's mother turned around from the sink. "What about you? Staying for breakfast?"

"Nah, I'll get something later. I need to get going. I'll see everyone later!" she replied.

Chell opened the front door, stepped out of her tiny house, and strolled over to her red bicycle that lay on the front lawn. She picked it up, placed herself on the seat, and began to pedal. As she zoomed down the poorly kept road, Chell's mind wandered back to the dream. Never had she experienced anything like that before. Yes, she would get nightmares often, as a child and even up until now, but this? Never had she had a dream so vivid and precise. The girl could remember the exact scene, the exact dialogues, the exact feeling. This dream didn't fade into the distance with time unlike most dreams.

Ten minutes later, the outline of the school's bell tower came into view. Chell increased her speed; she wanted to go into the courtyard as soon as possible. She had matters to discuss and people to discuss them with.

III

MEETINGS

Chell wheeled up next to the school courtyard and dismounted her bike. As the girl searched for her friends, she could hear a steady, didactic voice coming from up ahead.

"Ah, crap. Not them. It's too early for this," she groaned as she neared the responsible party.

In the large, open cobblestone courtyard surrounded by classrooms, a mass of people had gathered around a pale, black-clad boy who was perched on a crate and waving an ominous finger at the crowd. She ducked to avoided detection, but was confronted by another problem. Nearby, a wide-eyed girl sporting a large golden cross around her neck broke from a second mob and latched tightly onto Chell's sleeve. She thrust herself into Chell's face and stared; a mad fire burned in her eyes.

"You! Have you heard? Have you heard the news? It's coming, I tell you. The end is near! All of the signs point to it! The books were right!" she ranted, spraying Chell with saliva.

"Get the hell off me," Chell growled as she shook herself loose from the girl's grasp. She quickened her pace and thought about the two factions responsible for all the hysteria.

She didn't know which group she hated more: the Doomwatchers or the Repenters. The Doomwatchers looked for signs and symbols that told of the world's annihilation and made it their business to relay their prophecies to anyone and everyone in the vicinity. The Repenters believed that the Crisis was a foreshadowing of

Armageddon and that all must beg God's forgiveness for their sins. In Chell's opinion, they were both insane and she tried to avoid them as much as possible. However, no one could deny the existence of the Crisis, and almost everyone had their share of foreboding.

The ancient school loomed overhead as the girl scanned the dusty courtyard for her companions. Spotting them, Chell made her way through the torrent of students, hoping to avoid the Doomwatchers' voluminous predictions.

"Hey, guys," Chell said as she approached two of her friends. They broke from their conversation and turned to view the newcomer.

"You're here!" Chell's best female friend said, giving her a small hug. Her name was Katarina, but everyone called her Kitty for short. She was tall, with flaxen hair and a well-formed figure. Her eyes were colored like ferns, unlike Chell's jade ones. She and Chell had known each other for ages.

"Hey, girl. What's shakin'?" said the other girl, Serene. She had a personality that contradicted her name. She was loud and outgoing. While she was shorter than both Chell and Kitty, she had an attitude ten feet higher.

The girls waited for the final member of their group. Sure enough, a boy walked over to Chell's side.

"Good morning, everyone," he said with a grin. Axel was thin and was the same skin tone as Chell. His phthalo blue eyes sparkled in the morning sun. His straight black hair was well-groomed and his clothing reflected his alluringly refined taste. Chell could feel the heat rising to her cheeks as he playfully rested his arm on her shoulder.

"Anything interesting happened last night?" Axel directed towards the other girls.

"Nothing. Nothing important, anyway," Serene responded casually.

"What about you, Kitty? Anything to report?"

"Negatory. Oh! I did need to talk to you. About a project for humanities." With the last line, Kitty shot Axel a look, but Chell did not notice it.

Axel nodded slowly. "Yeah. Sure, I'll help," he said. He then looked over at Chell. "What about you, m'lady? Anything new?"

Before Chell could say anything, Kitty laughed. "Well, it's practically written all over her face; seems like somebody is just bursting to get something out! Come on, Chell, what deep, philosophical thought are you so earnest to share?" she teased.

Chell grinned but quickly grew serious. She looked around to make sure no one else was close enough to hear. "You'll probably think I'm insane when I finish, but I'm gonna tell you anyway. Last night, I had this weird dream. I walked down this really long, dark tunnel. When I finally reached the end, there was this crazy witch woman who was just sitting there, as if she had been waiting for me. Behind her was a huge door, all carved and expensive-looking. She told me I could either go through the door and see the future, or stay in the tunnel and live my life the way it is. Naturally, my dream-self chose to go through the door. But when I went through…"

She paused, frowning at the recollection.

"Go on, Chell," Axel urged her, surprised but intrigued at the same time.

"When I went through the door, it was as if all hell had broken loose. I was suddenly in some city, but it was on fire; buildings were crumbling, bodies were scattered all over the ground, people were running and screaming. Then, to make things worse, these massive tanks started rolling in."

"Tanks?" Kitty asked her.

"I guess they were tanks. There were about five of these huge pieces of machinery. People ran like hell to get away, but this little kid toddled in front of it, trying to reach his mother. The woman must have twisted her ankle or something because she limped towards him. She grabbed him, but before she could run, the tank thing blew both of them up. Her head landed at my feet. Then, I woke up," she finished with a shudder as she surveyed the group, awaiting their reactions and their advice.

The other three looked around at each other before Serene answered, "I'm no good with dreams, hon. The best I can tell you is don't worry 'bout it. It might be one crazy dream, but it's still a dream."

"I don't know," Chell said dubiously. "I still feel like this was more than a dream. It had more--Kitty, what's up? You look like your dog was tested for rabies and failed."

The group looked at Kitty, who had a worried frown etched deeply onto her face. "Chell, you are absolutely sure that this was what you saw?" Kitty asked with apprehension.

"Yeah, I'm sure," Chell answered, taken aback by the question.

"Positive? I mean, you haven't watched or read anything that could have influenced you in any way?"

"No, I'm positive."

The flaxen-haired girl bit her lip and seemed to contemplate her next comment.

"Chell, was there a logo on the killing machines? Any sort of special insignia?"

"A what?" the other girl asked, taken aback by the odd question.

"An insignia, Chell. Did you see an insignia?" Kitty asked with more intensity.

"Yeah, I guess there was an insignia. A blob...actually, I think it might have been a flame...but there were crossed swords at its base and a skull in the middle..." Chell said with a frown as she tried to understand the importance of it all.

"And you have no clue as to what that means?" Kitty asked slowly, her breathing greatly slowed.

"No, not at all! Kitty, what is this about?" Chell answered.

"Chell, come with me. I need to talk to somebody," Kitty said seriously.

Chell was surprised, but before she could say anything, the other girl grabbed her arm and pulled her firmly. The rest of the group followed closely behind.

"Kitty, you don't think she's--"Axel began.

"That's what I'm going to find out," Kitty called out as she continued to drag Chell along the outside of the circular courtyard. Chell looked behind at Axel questioningly but he only gave her a look of concern. Suddenly, Kitty halted in front of doorway that led to the school's interior.

"Wait here," she said before hurrying down the dark passageway.

Chell obeyed the command, too bewildered by her friend's strange behavior to question or protest. Not too far away, she could hear the boy she had seen earlier giving a passionate speech.

"Listen, all of you!" the crier said as he called to the hordes of students before him. "We must prepare for what is to come! The ancient texts speak of a dreamer, one who could see what is to come! What is to become of us! The dreams they see are the truth!"

Chell stiffened. She turned towards the speaker, waiting to hear more.

"Oracles, they are, gifted with powers of foresight! The Dreamers have seen the ways of the world! And what they see will *happen!*" he said.

Darkness swooped before her eyes and the world spun. The sense of falling flooded Chell's mind.

IV

RESURRECTION

Chell murmured to herself, turning her head, trying to make sense of the cushioned environment she was surrounded in. She could hear voices around her.

"I think she's awake!" a girl hissed. Chell pegged it as Kitty's.

"She will be now, idiot," Axel said coolly.

"You're calling *me* an idiot?" Kitty whispered.

"Yeah, he did. Are you deaf?" Chell heard Serene say.

"All of you. *Shut up*," Chell exclaimed, eyes still closed. She opened them and saw her friends crowded around her. She sat up and looked around what appeared to be the nurse's office.

"What happened?" she asked the group.

"You fainted," Axel answered.

"Axel caught you," Serene added with a cheeky wink. Axel blushed but his eyes gleamed when he looked at Chell.

"Ah, Ms. Greene. I see you're awake," a voice called from the doorway. In came a tall middle-aged man with a serious face and graying hair.

"Oh, wonderful. He's here. Chell, this is Dr. Lewinski," Kitty informed them, gesturing.

"Hello," Chell murmured cautiously, wondering what the man wanted from her.

The man drew up a chair and sat down next to her bed. Chell looked on calmly, not wanting to show her concern. The doctor studied her in silence as his eyes darted from one part of her face to another. Serene and Kitty sat down while Axel leaned against the back corner of the room.

Dr. Lewinski opened his mouth. "I have been informed that you have been having dreams of a peculiar nature, yes?" he inquired, pulling out a pad and pen.

"Er, yes. I have," Chell answered, confused as ever.

"About what?" he asked as he began to jot down notes.

"Doomsday. Death. Destruction," Chell intoned automatically. Flashes of the dream darted through her mind like scenes from a grisly accident.

"Would you mind telling me your dream? That is, if you can remember most of it," he asked politely. Chell retold her dream for the second time, withholding no details. Dr. Lewinski wrote down everything she said.

Chell watched as he scribbled on the yellow piece of paper before him. "Are you from some mental hospital or something? Because I'm not crazy," she blurted out, her eyes narrowed.

"No, Chell, I am not here to cart you away to an asylum. I am here to determine whether or not you are genuine," he said, not looking up from his paper.

"Whether or not I'm a genuine *what*?"

Giving no answer, he set the pen and paper aside, reached down, and put a black medical bag on his lap. He opened it and brought out a small glass vial filled with a purplish liquid. "Here, child, drink this. It won't harm you, trust me. This will help me determine if this was just a dream or something else." Dr. Lewinski persuaded her, handing Chell the liquid.

Chell took the glass vial and uncorked the bottle. She eyed the liquid inside warily, then drained the entire thing. It had a bittersweet taste, like dark chocolate, but was light and floral at the same time. *An odd combination,* thought Chell.

She looked at the man again, but he was taking more notes. "Do you feel anything?" he asked.

"No. Was I supposed to feel something?"

"An intense feeling of warmth, followed by a chill."

"Oh, well then. My body didn't get that memo," Chell muttered.

"Hm. This is no common dream," he noted as he went back to writing.

Chell looked at her friends. Serene shrugged, not knowing what to say. Axel and Kitty both smiled.

"Ok," Dr. Lewinski sighed, getting everyone's attention. "I want you to answer a few questions for me. Ready?"

"Yes," Chell replied, nodding.

"What color and style were the mysterious woman's clothes?"

"Midnight blue, with a black hem. Her robe was long, so it should have touched the wet floor, but it just floated above the water."

"Good. Were the two of you alone?"

"There were these ugly, fat mice in the tunnel, so I guess you wouldn't say we were *completely* alone."

"Good." He wrote down more notes. Chell could see that Kitty was becoming more and more worried.

"Would you be so kind as to retell the entire dream? And with every detail: the clarity of the water, the designs on the door, the length of the mother's hair, all of it." And Chell did, down to every last crack in the wall. Dr. Lewinski wrote down all that she said.

"Well, then," he announced, looking more at Kitty than at Chell. "I think we can all agree that this young woman is a genuine VOF."

Serene let out a small gasp and put her hand to her mouth. Kitty sighed with her head in her hands. Axel's expression was indecipherable.

"I'm a what?" Chell asked before realizing how stupid she sounded.

"*Videntis orbis fini*," Axel answered grimly. "Latin for 'one who sees the end of the world.' The tales of them have existed for ages, but only a few have ever emerged to be genuine. Even fewer lived to be right. People usually sent them into exile or executed them for heresy."

"Lived to be right? But the world hasn't ended before," Chell said.

"That's because they all pointed to a time well into the future: roughly around this year," Dr. Lewinski muttered. "The visions were always the same: images of a great city in flames with 'great beasts of steel' killing everyone in their path with 'stones of death' and 'scarlet lightning' raining down, as one Turkish VOF wrote down back in the 12th century."

"There was one in Pompeii who had these visions; he escaped the eruption of Mount Vesuvius, but when he started talking about his visions, the officials of the city he took refuge in linked it to Pompeii's destruction and had him tried and executed for sorcery. Luckily, someone kept his diaries after his death and they were copied a couple of times over the years. Another one was in China, a woman. She envisioned the same thing. Unfortunately for her, the 1556 Shaanxi earthquake came by and killed over 800,000 people. She was accused of witchcraft for the emperor thought she had brought about the quake, but she killed herself before they got to her. There was a Polish man who came out right before the start of WWII. Told his dream to a neighbor, who told a doctor and family friend. The man refused medical treatment and fled the country, assuming different names to get out of Europe during the war. Last thing we know is that he disappeared somewhere in Kazakhstan. But his dream was the same as the Shaanxi woman, and hers was the same as the Pompeian prisoner," said Kitty, who stood up and paced.

"So this wasn't just some crazy dream that I just happened to have?" Chell asked the doctor.

"No. That liquid that you drank was a serum that clears the mind of almost all illusions and visions; it is often used for drunkards, schizophrenics, or people with hallucinosis. However, true visions cannot be erased by any tonic. We discovered that about one hundred years ago when a man emerged from some obscure African village, ranting on about death and destruction. The vision had driven him insane, you see. He was given the serum and it changed nothing. We knew then that the VOFs were coming back and we've been looking for new ones ever since. We always hoped that more would emerge as the time of greatest need approached," Dr. Lewinski replied.

"Does the government know about this? The VOFs, I mean?"

"Bah, the government. Sure, they know about it. They should have paid more attention to it sooner, but as with anything, it always takes a massive civilian death toll or the death of their own before they realize something's amiss. But now they're so wrapped up with their political conquests, chasing after spies that don't exist and picking fights with countries they should be standing with. It's our job to pursue this stuff because we're the only ones capable."

"Who are 'we', exactly?" Chell asked.

The doctor shot a look at Kitty, who nodded slowly in response.

"Perhaps Katarina will address that at a later time. Right now, the main focus is you and your vision," Dr. Lewinski said. Chell obliged.

"So, whatever my dream was, it's going to happen?" she inquired, fearful of the answer.

"Most likely," the doctor replied with a sigh.

"Well, now what? Do I get locked up, or do I get worldwide respect and deity status?" Chell asked.

"Neither. None of the outsiders are to know of this," the man spoke seriously, looking at her from over his rimless glasses.

"Outsiders, sir?" Chell asked, weary of these new and confusing terms.

Another look towards Kitty, but also to Serene and Axel as well. Chell grew increasingly suspicious that her friends all knew something--whatever that something may be--that she didn't.

"Anyone outside this group here and your legal guardians, Chell," Dr. Lewinski answered.

"Alright."

Axel said grimly, "The rest of the world will know soon enough. There's no need to inform them before the time is right."

Dr. Lewinski nodded. "He's right; they will know eventually. The events that you surveyed in your dream will start to reveal themselves in the very near future."

At the sight of Chell's alarm, the man said, "'Tis an inevitable fact of life. It has been since the onset of the Crisis. With all of the financial turmoil and corruption and...other threats that emerged a century and half ago, it was only natural that things would only get worse before they get catastrophic. What we are facing now is merely a ripple from the initial events. The surge is yet to come."

He paused before continuing softly, "We never thought we would get here. We thought that these visions would die out and be exposed as just another manifestation from the minds of madmen and women. But your vision is proof, Chell. You are the last VOF, the final prophecy-bearer. I'm sure of it. That makes you very valuable, my dear. Very valuable indeed. And, if you were to fall into the wrong hands, the consequences could be paramount." He gave her a warning look and Chell nodded slowly.

The doctor turned to the rest of the group. "I would love to say that these killing machines will appear months from now. The truth is, though, they can show up on our doorsteps tonight, or this very instance, in fact." At this last statement, Serene gave an involuntary shudder. "We simply don't know," Dr. Lewinski concluded.

The room was silent as everyone digested this chilling news. Serene's earth-toned eyes darted from one person to the next, waiting for someone to speak. Kitty and Axel both stood solemnly and studied the lines on the floor.

Chell hated awkward silences and set to breaking this one at once. "Well then, there's no point in sitting around all day. I don't think the nurse will have any objections," she said as she dragged herself off of the bed. She was still slightly unsteady, so Kitty rushed to grab her arm. She turned to the middle-aged man and said, "I think it's high time that we go out into the world and face annihilation and the destruction of humanity. Maybe have a cup of coffee while we're at it."

"Sounds fine to me," Axel said as he stood up straight. "Serene, tell the nurse we'll be going, please." As Dr. Lewinski got up from his chair, he said, "You seem to be taking this rather well, Ms. Greene!"

Chell smiled and Axel replied, "Ah, Doctor. I think I speak for Chell when I say this: I would rather face Death head-on and with a smile than to cower in the shadow of His oncoming blade."

The doctor raised an eyebrow but nodded solemnly, and the procession filed out of the infirmary. The group of students continued through their normal day, trying to push the grim tale of the world's future into the recesses of their minds. Kitty, however, could not, and was busy formulating the steps that needed to be taken, and needed to be taken fast.

Meanwhile, Chell was left to ponder. Why was the insignia significant? What were the others hiding from her? A nagging feeling in her stomach told Chell that she was going to find out quite soon.

V

DISCOVERY

The day wore on and the conclusion of Chell's last class finally arrived. She biked home, rehearsing the lines she would tell her parents so as not to worry them. When she got home and walked into the kitchen, however, she knew she wouldn't have to say anything. The moment she set her bag down on the floor, her mother flew at her from the kitchen and wrapped her arms around her daughter. Chell embraced her mother back, stunned.

"You know?" Chell asked simply.

"Yes. A Dr. Lewinski called us. Why didn't you tell us about the dream?" Chell's mother replied, releasing her daughter at last.

"I didn't have time to. It would have taken too long to explain," Chell answered.

Chell's father emerged from the kitchen and gave his daughter a quick squeeze.

"So it's true? The Crisis is only the beginning? Something is coming?" he asked, hoping his daughter would say otherwise.

Chell put on a sad smile. "'Fraid so."

Her father sighed and shook his head. "We should have seen this coming," he muttered more to himself than aloud.

Chell tried to console her father. "There was no way anyone could've seen this--" The girl stopped short. "Dad, what do you do?"

"What do you mean, Chell?" he inquired.

"I mean, what do you do for a living?" his daughter questioned with a trace of suspicion in her voice.

"Well, I'm an engineer, honey. You know that," her father replied. She could see that he was avoiding her eyes.

"I know, but what sort of engineer and who do you work for?"

He smiled. "You sound like the FBI." Chell looked at him expectantly, waiting for his answer.

The man scratched his head and sighed. "Well, I don't exactly know where to start."

Chell's suspicions deepened. "Are you hiding something? Is there something about your work that I should know about?"

Chell's mother moved forward, scowling. "Chelsea, there is no need to interrogate your father this way. His work is his work. He is not obligated in any way to share—"

"Marie," Chell's father responded softly, turning to his wife. "Chell is no longer a child. She's capable of understanding, more now than ever before. I think it's safe to tell her."

He looked back at his daughter and opened his mouth to speak. He didn't get to explain, however, for at that moment the phone rang. Chell, being nearest to it, picked it up.

"Hello?" she said into the receiver. A familiar voice greeted her.

"Chell, this is Kitty. I need to talk to you. Can I come over?" the voice inquired. Chell detected a hint of urgency in her voice.

"Uh, sure. Like, right now?" Chell asked.

"Yes. Now."

"You sure this can't wait? I'm sort of in the middle of--"

"Chell, please. You need to know, for your own sake. Besides, Lewinski will kill me if I don't tell you."

"Tell me what? What's with all the secrecy all of a sudden?"

A pause ensued. "It would be better if I told you in person, given the nature of the information," Kitty uttered slowly.

"Okay. I'll be waiting outside." With that, she hung up the phone. Chell turned to her parents.

"That was Kitty. She wants to talk about...God knows what. Something about my dream," she explained. Her voice then grew hard. "Look, if you don't want to tell me, fine. You two wouldn't be the first ones to be keeping secrets from me. I just hope that whatever everyone is so keen on protecting is worth it in the end."

With that, she walked out of her house and sat on the front steps. Ten minutes later, she saw her friend's bike come whizzing up the street. Kitty came to a halt in front of the peeling, white picket fence, swung her leg off of her bike, and opened the gate. Kitty wheeled her bike inside, closed and locked the gate, and set her bike down on the grass. Chell rose from the steps, and with her head she motioned for Kitty to follow her into the backyard. Kitty nodded and walked behind her friend.

Both of the girls sat at the rectangular tile table on Chell's miniscule patio. At first, Kitty was silent, her head bowed and her lips tense. Chell waited to hear what Kitty had come to tell her, but

Kitty looked up at the sky and sighed. Chell grew impatient at her friend's delay, so she prompted Kitty to speak.

"Kitty, I know you didn't just come here to examine the clouds. There must be something you wanted to tell me that you couldn't say over the phone, so be out with it," Chell said with a hint of annoyance.

Kitty's eyes rested on the sky for a few seconds longer before she gave another deep sigh. She looked at Chell with a mix of pity, sadness, and anguish. "God, how do I start? It's all so complicated," Kitty said, shaking her head dolefully.

"How about you start at the beginning?" Chell suggested with mock kindness.

The blonde girl smiled, but her smile quickly vanished as she began her tale. "Throughout human history, there have been tales of domination, world annihilations, the works. However, none of these have ever been true."

"Obviously."

"Well, this time it's different. The time of mass destruction, epic wars, and great fires: it's coming."

Chell smiled grimly. "Of all people, you tell *me* this? Wasn't I the one who confirmed this?"

Kitty smiled and nodded. "Like Dr. Lewinski said, you did confirm that the time is finally here, but we have about two dozen accounts since the Early Dynastic Period of Ancient Egypt."

Chell's eyes narrowed. "You keep saying 'we'. You and Lewinski both. Who are 'we'?"

Kitty bit her lip, and Chell realized that her friend had misspoken. The dark-haired girl leaned forward, eyes still narrowed. "Kitty, who are they?" she asked, with more force this time.

Kitty gazed at Chell sadly, then sighed. She knew she would regret what she was about to divulge.

"Chelsea, it's not that easy," Kitty whined.

"I don't care. Tell me anyway." Chell replied firmly, crossing her arms across her chest and leaning back into her chair. "I'm ready."

Defeat flooded Kitty's eyes and she began her story.

"As you and the rest of the world know, the situation commonly referred to as 'the Crisis' started years ago. At that point, the stock markets of the world crashed and a worldwide recession hit. Poverty and starvation soon followed, but food and monetary shortages around the world meant little aid could be given. I don't think a single country was spared from hunger-related deaths. Following that, there were many accounts of countries sending spies to other countries because they suspected corruption. A couple of nations discovered the spies, and had them and their associates kidnapped, tortured, and brutally murdered. Images and videos became public and outrage swept across the face of the earth. Thus, the superpowers of the world were consistently on high alert and national suspicions escalated into open animosity. Assassinations followed suit, which also severed many of the alliances built between nations. World wars were always and still are a looming threat. Smaller countries were plunged into civil wars and guerilla violence. I'm sure you've seen the news."

Chell rolled her eyes. "Kitty, I know all of this already. Spare me the history lecture and tell me where you and I fit into this," she said.

Kitty paled slightly when Chell said 'you and I', but gave in.

"Ok, ok. I'll skip to the important part. Amid all of the turmoil, a new group was growing in power. They call themselves 'The Order of Shadows'. Their ideology is that the human race has become too weak and corrupt for it to continue going the way it is. So, they want a new world order to rise from the ashes. As they've said, 'from the darkness shall spring forth the light.'"

"That explains the shadowy cloud, then," Chell said, more to herself than anyone else.

"Yes."

"How big is this group, exactly?"

"They're probably a couple hundred thousand strong."

"Ok, so this is no small-scale rebellion we're talking about, then?"

"Not in the slightest. Problem is, the members of the Order aren't just common people with an opinion; we suspect that there are generals, financiers, weapon-dealers, strategists, scientists, governors, even presidents involved. Though they haven't launched a global attack yet, many lives have been lost because of them."

At this point Kitty got up and began to pace back and forth. "There have been tons of rebel groups in the past, but this one is different. They're extremely organized, well-trained, and elusive. It's so hard to find them, even though there are so many of them. They blend in like chameleons. And they're fast, too. By the time we're actually able to respond to an assassination or a bombing, the ones responsible are out of sight; there are no traces of them or their plans. The only evidence that there was a plan to kill anyone is the bodies of the victims. They have impeccable training.

Chell raised an eyebrow. "Then how do you know it's them?"

"Usually, the assassin will burn the Order's mark into its victim's flesh, or carve it in with a knife or some other gruesome act. Those weapons are never found. They're smart; they don't usually use guns because bullets can be traced. With blades or poison or fire or hazardous fumes, it's much harder."

"But you can still track them, can't you?"

Kitty shook her head. "They hide all of the evidence so well, it seems almost unnatural. Their strategy is phenomenal; their plans, no matter how large they may be, all fit together like cogs. Also, the 'Shadow-dwellers', as we call them, are brilliant actors and actresses. The reason that we can't find them is because they don't give any indications of being sadistic killers."

Chell thought for a moment, leaning further back into her chair. "These Shadow-dwellers must be very tightly knit with the powerful people of the world, including those who do not share their views."

"Correct. And it is very hard to determine who is part of the Order and who isn't. There is no special dress or tattoo that defines them. I mean, they must have their own ways of knowing who is friend and who is foe, but we don't know what it is." Kitty answered, placing her hands behind her back.

The girl grimaced as she continued, "We know very little about them. We don't know who they are specifically, who's running the show, who's financing them, who's supplying the weapons, who's covering them up...in short, we know virtually nothing about them. And they seem to know everything about us."

Chell was quiet for a moment. "Ok, so we have a wide-scale group of terrorists that wants to destroy us all and have managed to elude all forms of detection. Are you telling me that the people that are controlling the killing machines in my dream are Shadow-dwellers?"

"Yes."

"And the whole fire and death and world decimation is going to be by their hand?"

"Most likely."

"Great."

Both girls were silent as they absorbed this realization. Chell spoke up first. "So, what's my role in this? What's *your* role in all of this?"

"The countries that still had ties with each other became aware of this group after a series of assassinations, murders, and bombings. The Shadow-dwellers, feeling confident with their success, began leaving their marks. They sent messages to the great leaders of the world, finally making their existence known; however, they still kept themselves almost completely hidden," Kitty answered.

"Why didn't the countries do anything then?"

"Oh, they tried. They really tried. But by the time that the Shadow-dwellers came out into the world, they were very powerful. So, instead, they created an anti-terrorist group called 'The Society of Light.' Their job is to defend against and eventually destroy the Order of Shadows."

Chell looked alarmed at the mention of the word 'destroy', so Kitty added, "Not that type of destroy, but disband them, convert the ones that could be converted, imprison the ones who can't. Execute the ones who are running the show."

"You work for the Society of Light?"

"I'm a recruiter, but if I'm needed to fight, I can fight. That's what we want you to be."

Chell was silent and looked away from her friend. Kitty sensed that the girl needed convincing.

"Chell, the Order of Shadows would do anything to get their hands on you. You are a confirmation that their plans can work. If they know that they could be successful, they could start their campaign of terror sooner and possibly use you to find ways to improve their tactics. Who knows what else they'll do."

The girl shook her head as she attempted to clear the thoughts that crammed her brain.

Kitty leaned in closer to her friend, staring hard into her eyes. "The Society will offer protection to you and your family."

"Jesus, Kitty. Let me at least tell my parents!"

"They already know."

"How?" Chell asked in disbelief.

Kitty pursed her lips together. "Never mind that. But they already know of this proposal, and will have no issue if you choose to accept it."

Chell looked at her friend. *More secrets. There must be a catch,* Chell thought to herself. *But what more can I do?* She shook her head in defeat; Kitty interpreted this as a sign of uncertainty and prepared another round of persuasive words. Before she could begin, however, Chell held up her hand.

"I need to think about it, Kitty. Just...let me think about it," she said.

Seeing that she could not coax an answer out of her friend now, Kitty decided to leave the subject alone. She reached across the table, took Chell's hands in hers, and gave them an affectionate squeeze. She then got up and quietly left. Chell remained in her seat, contemplating.

Her thoughts were interrupted half an hour later by another visitor.

"Hello there, Chell," a smooth male voice said. Chell looked up to find Axel crossing her yard. She smiled at him.

"Hey. What're you doing here?" she asked him casually.

"I came over to check on you." he replied. "Do you mind if I sit?"

"Of course not!" she said, pointing to a chair near her. He lounged in it and turned towards her.

"How are you so far? You've been through quite a lot today."

"I'm doing better. It's a bit of a shock still, but I'm getting better."

"I can imagine. That's one crazy dream, and for all of it to be coming true...I just never thought it would happen in our lifetime."

"Tell me about it. I knew the Crisis was bad, but not *that* bad."

They sat in reflective silence for a little while before Axel spoke.

"Did Kitty come and talk to you?" he asked, a slight hint of suspicion in his voice.

"Uh, yeah. She just came to check on me, much as you're doing now," she replied. Although she trusted Axel, she felt as though she shouldn't tell anyone about the Society proposition until she made a decision.

"Oh, well that's good," he said nodding, satisfied with her answer. He got up to leave. "Take a couple of days off, Chell. I'm serious;

you need a break. I'm sure the teachers would understand, even if they don't know about the Dream."

"What about you and Kitty and Serene? I won't be able to see you guys," Chell asked.

"We'll come to see you. I promise," he responded. He took her hand into his and planted a small, soft kiss on her fingers before departing. Chell rejoiced silently in her mind.

Once Axel had gone from sight, Chell got up and went back into the house.

"Dad? Dad!" she called, pausing to hear a response.

"Yeah?" came a faint reply.

"Can we finish our little discussion, please?"

"...honey, I'm doing some work in the attic. That'll have to wait."

"Dad, can't we do that now? It's impor--"

Her words were interrupted by a loud thud, most likely the result of a dropped hammer. Chell sighed and went to her room.

The girl took Axel's advice and stayed home for a couple of days. The others visited her every day. Kitty said nothing about her offer, but the look in her eyes made it apparent that she wanted to. Chell was determined to think it through before acting.

A few days of deliberation passed before she came to her conclusion. She arrived in front of Kitty's house one afternoon. It was a small, white establishment with red shutters and a white door. She rang the doorbell and waited for her friend to appear. Sure enough, Kitty answered the door.

"Have an answer for me?" Kitty asked quietly.

"Let me make this clear," Chell responded. "We better be protected. I don't want anything happening to my family because of this. Can you assure me that the Society will protect my loved ones?"

"Don't worry, Chell. We'll make sure nothing will happen," Kitty said.

Chell nodded to herself, her mind finally at ease.

"So," she said, "When do I start?"

VI

DOUBTS

"Axel, you can't."

"I damn well can."

Rain struck hard against the windowpanes of Axel's house. The street outside was deserted save the occasional stray dog or wandering homeless person. Inside, Chell sat on a low sofa with her arms wrapped around herself as she worriedly watched Axel pace back and forth. The dim lights cast a dangerous shadow over his features as he agitatedly walked around the room.

"But why? I don't understand--"

"It's a sham, Chell. All of it. This whole 'let's make the world safe again' is a lie. Hell, the name itself is a lie."

"Axel, what do you mean it's a lie? The Society of Light was designed to--"

"Designed to be an anti-terrorist organization, yes, I know. Believe me, I was told the exact same thing that Kitty told you. That we're going to help people, that we'll be remembered in history as the saviors of mankind in its darkest hours. But I've been in it for long enough to know that's not true."

Axel slammed his empty whiskey glass on his drawing room table. Anger flashed in his eyes, but was soon replaced by anguish. He walked over to Chell and kneeled before her. He took her hands into his and looked into her eyes.

"They're not what you think they are, Chell. They really, really aren't. I know the stories--"

"And that's all they probably are, Axel! Stories!" she exclaimed. "Nothing more than malicious rumors!"

"You've been in, what, eight months? Believe me, I thought the same way about the Society my first eight months. But then I learned. They aren't just stories; I've seen it all! With my own eyes! Reprehensible things, Chelsea. Hell itself would never harbor such criminals," he groaned as he stood up again.

He grabbed the glass off the table and poured himself another drink from a crystal liquor decanter. He downed the whiskey in one shot and moved to pour some more, but Chell grabbed the decanter and moved it on the other side of the table.

"Look," she said as she stood to leave. "It's late, you've had a rough couple of months and you've been drinking. You obviously aren't in the fittest state of mind right--"

"Oh, damn the drink, Chell! I'm seeing things clearer now than I ever have," Axel blurted out as he moved towards her. He put both of his hands on Chell's shoulders. "I'm leaving, Chell. I'm leaving the Society. You *need* to leave, too."

"Axel, you know I can't do that. You know *you* can't do that! We made a commitment!"

"Things change. People change. I refuse to be part of the Society of Light any longer!" he said as his voice became shriller. His hands went to the side of her face as he put his forehead against hers.

"Come with me. I don't want to be apart from you," he said, his tone softer and more subdued.

"Don't be silly, I'm not going anywhere."

"Chell, this organization will tear us apart. All of your friends and loved ones will be tossed up in this giant divide between the forces of evil and eviler. Separated we will be, and by whom? Vile men vying only for profit and glory. We both know this. You have to leave. For me. For us. Please."

The lights flickered as the threat of a blackout grew with the storm's increasing intensity. Chell moved towards the doorway, but Axel quickly grabbed her hand.

"Don't go. Stay with me. You'll be safer here," he quietly begged.

Chell didn't respond. She broke away from his grasp, grabbed her coat from a chair, and walked out of the room. Axel stared after her, then turned towards the table and poured himself another drink. He moved to the window with the glass in his hand and watched Chell walk down the street until she rounded a corner and disappeared. He finished his whiskey.

****

More time passed before anything of importance happened to Chell, but international tensions, domestic violence, and economic downturn continued to escalate. It was late into August. The sun had reached its zenith in the azure afternoon sky, but its warming rays could not penetrate the cold, dark cloud of fear and uncertainty that hung over the world like a dense fog.

Amid this cloud, Chell lay stretched out on her bed and stared at the off-white ceiling above her, her hand on a large textbook and papers strewn at her feet. Her clock next to her bed ticked loudly with every second that passed. With an absent-minded glance at the clock, the girl sat up and planted her feet on the ground. As she sat on the edge of her bed, she massaged her throbbing temples, trying to dispel the troubled thoughts that inhabited her mind.

Chell stood up, walked out of her bedroom, and into the narrow hall. The door to her father's office, a place she and her brother had long been forbidden to enter, was closed, but light from under the door indicated that her father was on the other side. Her mother's car keys were missing from their usual hook, indicating that she had gone out on an errand. Chell stepped outside and gently closed the sliding glass door behind her.

Her brother was sitting outside, his knees pulled close against his chest. A gentle breeze blew, ruffling Jack's shaggy black hair. He stared up at the clouds, the floating cotton puffs taking on a multitude of formations up ahead. Chell sat next to him and they both stared on in silence. At last, Chell spoke up.

"Any particular reason why you're sitting out here all alone?" she asked him while still studying the sky. "It kind of feels like one of those cheesy romance movies when the girl sits by the beach and contemplates--"

"Shut up," Jack said, smiling. But he soon settled back into a gloomy silence. Moments passed and both seemed to be absorbed by the quiet that blanketed them. Then, Jack let out a deep sigh. "I don't know, Chell," he said as he turned to his sister. "I just feel that things aren't gonna get better. The Crisis is getting worse and worse every month. More people are dying. Already, two of my classmates were killed by gangs. More countries are preparing for war. I know that it'll all end eventually, but I don't think it's gonna end pretty."

Chell stared at her teenage brother. She remembered the way that she ruffled his hair the morning after her Dream. Over the past few months, she saw him transition from his usual happy, carefree self to the quiet, downcast person he was now. He was a recluse in his own mind, chained by his overcast thoughts. As his frown steadily grew, Chell put her arm around him.

"Hey. No point thinking about death and destruction. You'll get more grey hairs if you stress yourself out," she said, running her hands through his long black hair. "I don't have any...never mind," Jack said, grinning. He gave his sister a quick hug, stood up, and went inside the house. Chell watched him go, then continued to look up at the sky. Her peace was disturbed, however, by the vibrating phone in her pocket. She promptly answered it.

"Hello?" she asked.

"Hey, it's me." It was Kitty. "Can you come over? I've got a gift for you."

"Can't this wait?"

"Hey, it's a special gift. Are you sure you wanna turn it down?"

Chell scowled, but replied, "I'll be there." She shoved the phone back into her pocket and she walked back into her home. She went to the office door, knocked, and put her cheek against the wood.

"Dad, I'm going to Kitty's. I'll be back. I'm gonna pick something up," she said.

"Ok, honey. Come back soon," came the reply.

Chell decided to bike to Kitty's instead of driving, so she got her jacket, went outside, grabbed her bike, and swung her leg over it. She heard two loud taps from above her. The girl looked up and saw her brother looking at her from his bedroom window. He gave a melancholy smile and raised his hand up slightly in a wave. Chell smiled back and raised her hand in farewell, then turned around and pedaled onto the side of the road. Jack watched his sister bike down the road, tears welling up in his eyes and spilling down his cheeks. Far down below, Chell wiped away the brackish drops that flowed from her own eyes. In her mind, she could not determine its cause: whether it was the sting of the wind that caused her tears, or the anguished, hopeless look that now clouded her dear brother's face.

VII

GIFTS

Chell stopped in front of Kitty's house. Before Chell had even leaned her bike against the fence, her fair-haired friend opened the door and motioned for her to come in. Chell dashed up the stone steps and entered the house. She followed Kitty down a narrow hallway. At the far end of it, Kitty turned into her room, Chell following close behind. Chell had spent many afternoons in this room, but all of her visits did not prepare her for the sight she saw next. Kitty walked over to the large blue Persian rug in the center of the room and moved it aside. Under it was a circular door with the same designs as the rug. The girl unlocked it and a dim light flickered on from down below. Chell saw a ladder and could faintly make out the bottom of the secret room.

"You stay here." Kitty ordered, then she climbed down the ladder. Chell peered over the doorway's edge. She heard when her friend reached the bottom, and it seemed that Kitty was unlocking a trunk or a case. She was confused for a while until she heard the unmistakable sound of a bullet being loaded into a gun. "Oh, no. No no no no no. You've got to be kidding," the girl said as she backed away from the circular opening in the floor.

"I'm afraid not, my friend," Kitty said as she climbed back up the ladder. "Times are hard. Things are getting messy. Either you use it, or someone uses it on you." With that, she handed the girl a semiautomatic pistol. Chell took it, weighed it in her hand, and looked at it with slight disdain.

"I don't even know how to shoot this thing," she whined, trying to find a way out of using it.

"Chell, it's a Glock. How hard can it be? Point and shoot. Simple as that," she reassured her friend, miming the actions with another pistol she had brought with her.

Kitty motioned for Chell to follow her back outside. They left the house again and went into the garage. There, Kitty's car was parked. Guns still in hand, Kitty went into the driver's side and started the vehicle while Chell nervously sat in the passenger's side. As Kitty opened the garage door and backed out, Chell asked, "Where are we going?"

"You're going to need to learn how to shoot. We obviously can't do it here," she replied. Once she turned off of her property, Kitty sped down the road. Chell's stomach turned as she stole quick glances at the guns.

For fifteen minutes they drove until they finally came to the outskirts of a thick wood. The area had long been abandoned and the grounds were quite overgrown. Kitty parked the car and the two girls stepped out. While Chell warily eyed the dark trees, Kitty marched forward to a roughly-beaten path. Chell followed after her. They went far into the woods and the sun struggled to peek through the tall canopy. The area was silent except for the cawing of crows and the rustling of leaves. The wind whipped through the trees and made a soft, sad sound.

Finally, Kitty stopped and held her hand up to stop Chell from going further. She pointed into a clearing. "You see that big, ugly rock over there?" She motioned to a large boulder with her hand. "Shoot it."

Chell looked startled. "Don't worry so much! Point and shoot. Don't be so spineless," Kitty chided casually.

Chell swallowed, then aimed the gun at the rock. Her finger hesitated on the trigger for seconds, then she swiftly pulled it. A shot ran out through the forest, scattering the crows from the high treetops. Even from her distance, she could see the great crack that now marred the grey rock's surface.

"Wonderful!" Kitty said, beaming.

The flaxen-haired girl surveyed her friend as she stared out into the open. The area was quiet; Chell had yet to tear her eyes away from the rock. Instead, she raised her arm back up, aimed, and shot three consecutive shots at the already-damaged rock. Slowly, a smile crept on Chell's face. Kitty's heart skipped a beat; she thought that, just for the slightest second, she had spotted a mad glint in Chell's viridescent eyes.

"Chell?" Kitty asked warily, starting to worry. Her friend didn't answer. Kitty moved closer to her and gripped Chell's shoulder. The raven-haired girl jumped, as if she had woken from a trance. She turned to Kitty.

"Sorry. I just sort of...drifted." Chell's voice was far away, as she looked back to the fractured boulder.

Kitty looked over her friend with concerned, but a grin soon spread out on her face. "Hey, no worries. That gun is yours now," she said, but her features soon grew stern. "Now, Chell. This weapon is exactly what I said it is: a weapon. It's not a toy..."

"Oh, come on, Kitty. You aren't going to start with me on that, are you? What do you think I'm going to do? Shoot up the supermarket or something?" Chell cried out, appalled at Kitty's comment. Kitty let out a small sigh of relief as the uneasiness she had felt earlier quickly faded. She smiled and said, "Well, in time, you'll be getting a lot more than that. There are so many different types of guns, grenades, tactical knives..."

"Tactical knives?" Chell inquired, raising her eyebrows.

"Yeah, I've got some of those. Do...do you want one?" Kitty asked slowly, the uneasiness coming back to her.

Chell shrugged her shoulders. "Sure. You can never be too careful, I guess," she replied.

Their task completed, the two girls went back to the car and drove to Kitty's house. They returned to her room and she went down to the weapons hold. She retrieved a sheathed fixed blade knife and came back upstairs. She paled slightly at the sight of Chell's eager, outstretched hand, and Chell had noticed it, too.

"Kitty," Chell said with a laugh. "Don't worry about it. You can trust me with this thing. We've been friends since we were in diapers. You know me; I wouldn't do anything."

The blonde girl smiled, reassured once more.

"Don't worry about accuracy. We can practice that, and I'm sure you'll be getting plenty of field training soon enough."

Above, she could hear a squadron of fighter planes on approach and finally appear. Neither of the girls had paid much mind to it; these planes always flew overhead on constant patrol. Chell casually watched as they lifted away while Kitty spoke up.

"Then again, who knows? Maybe this whole Crisis thing will dissipate on its own and everyone will be safe and sound."

Chell rolled her eyes. "Kitty, that's so childish."

The words had barely left Chell's lips when a terrific blast broke the silence of the town. Screams and shouts rang out along the street; the chaos and fear from within the homes were audible. Chell let out a small shriek as Kitty grabbed her arm and manhandled her away from the window. Both of them waited, hearts racing and breaths short. Fear clouded their sight, and it was many moments before they could clearly see the vermilion haze off into the distance.

Kitty dashed to the window; she could hear a plane in the vicinity. Not long after, it came into view. Her eyes diverted once more to the red sky in the distance.

"Oh, my God, Kitty breathed to herself. Chell staggered to the window, her eyes wide open and fastened to the horrific blood-colored halo that pulsated in the background.

"Fire," she murmured to herself in a trance-like voice. Like a blind woman, she groped for her newly acquired weapons. She accidently knocked the gun aside but grasped the knife. She mumbled something about coming back and she raced out of the door and out of the house.

Barreling towards her bike, Chell swung her leg over the bar. She paid no attention as the chain sliced her leg. She steadied herself and began to pedal, faster and faster. The scarlet liquid flew off her leg like the drops flung off of a wet dog. The roads, the people, the bike she was riding: everything was a blur. Chell was intoxicated by a lethal concoction of fear and bewilderment. Her senses were put on mute and only her dire sense of urgency forced her body to move. She rounded the corner, the fiery haze growing ever stronger. The sight that met her stopped her heart and threw her off the bike.

The houses were ablaze. All along the road, the girl could see families and neighbors gathered, eyes filled with tears and wide with terror. The house that was the most damaged, however, was Chell's, and there was no one gathered in front of it. The little colonial-style house had turned into a raging inferno. The curtains flapped out of the broken windowpanes with ghost-like motions. Immense columns of smoke levitated up from the burning building. The siding was charred black and pieces of vinyl fell from the second floor. Cracking noises echoed the neighborhood as some of the beams gave way. Then, the roof caved in, sending sparks flying everywhere. They littered the yard and ignited little fires all over the grass.

Chell regained her sense to stand. With trembling hands and knees, she steadied herself and her bike. Like a brainless shell, she slowly trudged towards her former home. No tears, no mouth left agape, no sounds; just a remnant of a person marching ever closer. As she approached the monstrous pile of tinder, the flames grinned and acknowledged her presence. Chell stood dumbstruck as the flames teased and goaded her, leaping and lashing out in her face. Its deafening roar was like the malicious laughter of a villain; taunting and dripping with hate. The firefighters arrived by this time and called out to Chell. They yelled and they cautioned, but to no avail. To Chell, their vocal chords were severed; their mouths formed words, but they were incapable of sound. All she registered was the spiteful fire that beckoned to her like Lucifer.

Who had grabbed her, she didn't know. But Chell could feel that she was being whisked away from the collapsing bonfire. She didn't struggle, she didn't fight. The flames still enraptured her and filled her very being with a sense of hateful, sickening wonder. The thunderous laughter of the flames was like wax in her ears; they prohibited all other sounds from reaching the receptors of Chell's mind.

But one.

My name is being called, Chell thought to herself. It was true. A voice pierced through the earsplitting roar of the fire; a voice that Chell knew and loved. Like a newborn kitten, she stumbled blindly towards it, her only salvation. An intense sense of relief flooded though her as she came in contact with the only person available to her now.

Nothing mattered to Chell. Nothing else mattered other than her mother clutching at her. Her warmth flooded through the girl, as did her tears. Both women sobbed and held each other, unwilling, almost unable to let go. Seconds seemed like hours and the agony continued.

"Madame. Madame." The embrace was broken by the interruption of a police officer. They both gazed at him with glistening, vacant eyes. The officer colored when he realized how bad his timing was. But he continued, "Madame, I'm sorry to inform you that both your husband and son have died in the fire. We have located the bodies and are working to retrieve them."

Chell's mother stared at the officer, her face ashen and her eyes dead. In the background, the firefighters were dousing the flames. Neither mother nor daughter said a word, while the young cop's color slowly matched the hue of his tomato-soup hair. Suddenly, Chell's mother opened her mouth and said in a shuddering calm, "T-thank you, officer." With that, she sat on the sidewalk with her head between her knees. She began to rock slowly as her body shuddered with fresh sobs.

The officer seemed at a loss for words. He looked at Chell, opened his mouth, but thought better of it and closed it. Both just stood there, lost in thought. Without looking at him, Chell broke the silence and asked in a monotone voice, "How did the blaze begin?"

The officer started, extremely shocked by the question. "Um, well it...it was a...well, a bomb, miss." He stammered, searching for the right words.

"Did the Order drop the bomb?"

Again, surprise, then answers. "No, miss. It wasn't them. It-- and I wish it wasn't so--but it was the Society that dropped it! I saw the plane myself!"

The officer wanted to continue, but a look of fear clouded his face. He had said too much. The Society of Light wasn't something to be discussed with commoners. But he was confused. This girl seemed to know exactly what he was talking about. Exactly *who* he was talking about. "You...you know about them, miss?" he asked cautiously.

"Indeed officer, I do. I thank you for this information. You may continue with your work," Chell replied stoically.

The officer understood that he was dismissed and scurried away. Chell stood cemented on the sidewalk. She wanted to comfort her mother but could not will her body to move. Absently, she stuck her hands in her pocket. Her finger touched cold metal, so she pulled it out. The knife. Thoughts flooded into her head: of the knife, Kitty, the Society.

Kitty had said...she had said...good God, what did Kitty say? Chell thought in exasperation. She looked about for answers. The question gnawed at her. Then she saw two body bags being led from her remnant of a house. The first one was obviously her father; it was wide and long. The second bag's passenger was so slight that one person was carrying it bridal-style.

Chell remembered. Kitty had said the Society of Light will keep her family safe. Kitty said no harm would befall them.

Kitty lied. The Society lied. Kitty lied.

Chell crumpled to the ground wailing, emotion surging through her like a shockwave. She beat her hands against the ground and screeched to the sky. Tears raced down her face in torrents. Her cries were like those of a prisoner on a torturing rack: sheer, bloody agony. She felt as though her very existence was being cleaved in two. Chell punched the ground until her knuckles were raw and the pavement was stained with her blood. Her torment lasted for minutes, but it seemed like eternity: a bitter, godforsaken eternity. Finally, after being drained, Chell dragged herself towards her still-weeping mother. Her only thoughts consumed her, repeated over and over again with a growing intensity.

The Society lied.

They killed my family.

They lied.

They will pay.

VIII

ENIGMAS

"Here, take this. Drink the tea, dear. It'll make you feel better."

The café was warm and full of life, but for Chell and her mother, it was the stark opposite.

Accompanying them was Chell's grandmother. A kind-hearted old thing, she had taken in her daughter and granddaughter. She coaxed Chell's mother into accepting a mug of herbal tea.

"Thanks, Mom," the woman croaked, her voice hoarse.

"Anytime, Marie dear," the elderly woman replied, watching her daughter's every movement. She clasped and unclasped her hands under the table, her various gold bracelets clinked softly. Her ancient earrings poked out from under her fluffy mass of dove-white hair.

Chell let out a deep sigh and rested her head against the frosty glass window. She watched the world go about its daily business. A TV was playing in the café. Chell could see that the president was speaking, but she was unable to fully make out his words.

A bell indicated the arrival of new customers and drew Chell's attention away from the screen. Two men in long coats and sunglasses had entered. They scowled as they surveyed the area, but the other patrons paid them no mind. They turned towards

Chell and she could see the badges on the front of their coats, badges most of the world did not recognize. Her blood boiled. It was the badge of the Society of Light. Its silver logo--three pairs of wings holding a sword aloft--seemed to wink at her menacingly like a torture-happy warden. The girl gritted her teeth but did not tear her eyes away from the agents. They remained as if looking for something, but then soon left. Chell exhaled and watched them cross the street from her window. *They will pay soon enough,* she thought to herself. Chell got up from the table.

"I've got some things I need to take care of. For the Society." The last part Chell said through clenched teeth.

Chell's mother looked up at her, scared. "The Society? What do they want with you? Why--"

"Marie," Chell's grandmother interjected, cutting her daughter short. "Chell has work she must do. Regardless of...what happened three months ago, she still has a duty to uphold." She looked at her granddaughter, who nodded solemnly. *That's right,* Chell thought to herself, *I have a duty to uphold.*

Chell's mother looked at her surviving child with doleful eyes. Chell reached out and grasped her mother's hand, squeezing it gently. The air was tense with emotion, but at last Chell's mother nodded slowly. Chell smiled; she had gotten the go-ahead.

"Everything will work out, Mom," she reassured her. She planted a kiss on her mother's head and gave her grandmother a quick squeeze. She grabbed her purse and exited the café. Deciding to leave the car for her family, she walked down the street in the direction of her grandmother's house. "Everything will work out just fine." Chell murmured out loud.

****

Kitty studied the polished mahogany floor, trying to quell the storm-cloud of thoughts that were ravaging her brain. The gentle, upward motion of the elevator would have normally soothed her, but today she could find no comfort from it. She had too big of a job to do. Onwards the lift climbed, higher and higher every second. The little red numbers reached into the thirties, but they did not cease there.

"How like him," Kitty muttered under her breath, a grim smile playing on her lips. "Just to prove that he's on top of everyone else, he decides to have the entire fortieth floor to himself."

The elevator came to a sudden halt and the doors glided open. The giant office was bustling with people, and the sounds of ringing telephones, rustling papers, and intense conversations made the entire atmosphere seem like total chaos. Stepping out of the lift, Kitty clutched her papers and walked over to the high counter in front of her. Behind the counter, a petite, bespectacled woman was furiously writing down numbers while balancing two receivers on her shoulders.

Kitty waited patiently, not wanting to disturb the preoccupied woman. The receptionist's lithe hands zipped to and fro like excited bees, handing papers from one person to the next, shuffling folders, and looking up information. A few minutes passed before she looked up and saw Kitty. The receptionist put a hand over the phone receiver and whispered "Are you waiting for Mr. Harding?"

Kitty nodded. The woman pointed at a cluster of chairs off to the corner and said simply, "He'll be with you in a moment." Before Kitty could reply, the receptionist had replaced the phone by her ear. Murmuring a 'thank you' to her, Kitty walked away from the counter and proceeded to the area the woman had pointed out. She sunk into the highly-cushioned chair, but she could not fully relax. She was about to come face-to-face with one of the most powerful members of the Society of Light, and she was going to question him on matters greatly beyond her position.

The girl was lost in her thoughts for a long while before the polished chestnut door swung open. Two men stepped out and shook hands warmly. The younger of the two was definitely happy, for he left the office whistling to himself. Kitty's business, however, was with the elder. She stood up as he beckoned impatiently for her to come into his office. Kitty walked inside the richly decorated office, closing the door softly behind her. But she had little time to admire the paintings and wall fixtures, for she had much to discuss and did not want to waste time.

On the man's grand chestnut desk rested a brass name plate that read 'Joseph Harding'. He was a powerful executive who handled the Society's affairs. All unit mobilizations, demobilizations, attacks, retreats, and pretty much any other plans concerning the troops were approved by him. An average-looking man in his late fifties, he was conceited beyond measures and loved to make his position of power known to all around him. Among the lesser staff, besides all of his other vices, he was known to suffer from the three "M's": misogyny, misology, and misoneism.

Kitty grimaced mentally as she remembered the three M's. Lo and behold, she was fulfilling all three; not only had she failed his test by being a woman, she was also presenting him with an argument and reason, as well as asking for change. Already, she could see a sneer of contempt forming on his lips. Knowing that she may be denied an audience with him at any given moment, she opened her mouth to speak. However, Harding stopped her short with the raise of his wrinkling hand.

"Let me make myself very clear Miss...what did you say your name was?" he started, his deep voice echoing in the room.

"Katarina Johnson, sir," Kitty replied timidly.

"Ah, yes, Ms. Johnson. Like I said, I'm going to be very clear about this. I make the final decisions. All plans that come from my mouth are permanent unless I take it back. I've been here for thirty years and I had to fight all the way up here. I am the boss here; I make the decisions. So, once I make up my mind about something, it would be in your best interest not to question it. Am I understood?"

"Yes, sir."

Satisfied that his power had been established, he leaned back into his padded leather chair. "So, tell me, Ms. Johnson. Why are you here?"

Kitty inhaled and gathered her papers about her. "Well, sir," she started, "as you know, there were five bombs dropped three months ago on November 14. There were a total of six deaths in the process, and--"

Harding held a hand up to cut her short. "Ms. Johnson, I am fully aware of the situation; I executed it. But my question is why are you here? Surely it wasn't to give me a review of our operations."

Kitty flushed, but continued on. "No, sir. The reason I'm here today is because I want to know why."

"Why?" Harding asked, a small smile forming on his lips. "What do you mean, 'why'?"

"I mean, why were six innocent people killed by our group, especially since some of them are *part* of the Society?" Kitty replied with an edge of indignation. The ironic smile that played about Harding's lips irritated her beyond belief; he knew something that she didn't, and he was going to make every effort to let her know that.

"Ms. Johnson, do you realize what you are dabbling in? Do you *truly* know what you're dabbling in?" Harding asked her smoothly, the taunting in his voice barely disguised. Kitty swallowed her urge to give a spiteful retort and replied with a simple "Yes, sir, I do."

Harding slammed his massive hand on the desk, rattling his desk and Kitty's wits. "No, Ms. Johnson. You don't," he snapped. Harding stood up and walked over to the great floor-to-ceiling window that was behind his desk. Clasping his hands behind his back, he gave a self-satisfied smile and looked out at the bustling metropolis below him.

"Let's think for a moment, shall we, Ms. Johnson?" he said with a lofty air, still not facing the young woman. "Imagine what would happen if I told all of my subordinates why I execute certain plans the way I execute them. What do you think would happen?"

Kitty gritted her teeth at the mention of 'subordinate', but decided to humor the old man. "I don't know, sir," she replied, trying to keep the mockery out of her voice.

The man didn't catch her drift but saw her answer as the typical response of all idiotic women.

"Of course you don't," he said, finally turning towards the girl. "I don't have time to spell this out for you, Ms. Johnson, but let's put it this way. The bombings are not your concern. If they were your concern, you would already have received the information you seek. But since it is *not* your concern, you will either have to get your answers elsewhere, which I doubt you will be able to do, or you will have to forget all about this case." Harding leaned forward over the desk, his hawk-like eyes magnified by his glasses. "Drop this inquiry, Ms. Johnson. You are meddling in matters that are much too sophisticated for you." He emphatically spat this statement out at the young woman.

Unable to take the ridicule any longer, Kitty lashed out, malice dripping in her voice. "I think the death of a close friend's family concerns me. I think the decimation of private property concerns me. I think plaguing the family of a Society member with an onslaught of problems concerns me. *Sir.*" She interjected the last word with mock politeness.

Harding looked coldly at the girl for a few moments and the room was deathly silent. However, he merely shrugged his shoulders and leaned back into his chair.

"Your judgment has become clouded with emotion. I would have expected better from a Society member, regardless of your social stature. Regardless, I have the last say. There are no arguments. You will get no information that you do not need to have and you will abandon this case. My word is final, Ms. Johnson."

The contemptible man stood up and placed his hand on the polished brass doorknob of his office door. "I believe that our meeting is concluded, Ms. Johnson," he said coolly as he opened the door. Kitty glared at the executive and remained fixed in her seat, but she was aware that the rest of the floor was becoming curious, so she decided to leave. Gathering her papers, she stood up and smoothed her skirt. She walked past Harding without another word. However, he caught her wrist in a firm grip.

"Remember, Ms. Johnson," he hissed. "Everything I've said, everything I've done, everything I've decided; they've all been for the greater good. Do not forget that." His misty grey eyes stared hard into Kitty's green ones.

Kitty smiled sweetly at the man, but her voice was cool and precise. "For the greater good of whom, sir?" she asked in a hushed voice. She wrenched her arm free and began walking towards the elevator, not giving a second glance back. As the girl was hidden from sight by the silvery doors of the lift, Harding shook his head.

****

Kitty fumed silently as she waited in the elevator again. A sense of failure washed over her like a deluge. Here she was, standing in the exact same place as thirty minutes ago, yet she had accomplished nothing. Kitty had known that Harding would have been difficult, but not *that* difficult. She had hoped that she could get something out of this meeting; however, all she gained was frustration and more questions.

Finally, the lift reached the lobby and everyone bustled out. Kitty shook her head to clear the rampant thoughts and dug into her purse for her ID card; she wouldn't be allowed to leave without having her card scanned, lest she be some imposter who had miraculously avoided detection the first time. No one was behind her at the check post, so she stopped to converse with the woman at the counter.

"Hello, Kitty. It seems that your meeting with Mr. Harding was productive," she commented sympathetically, noting the dissatisfied look on the girl's face.

"Ah, yes. *Very* productive," she replied airily, her mind wandering as she had her card scanned. She watched as a bus boarded its passengers, preparing to leave.

No sooner had the last person stepped onto the bus when a fiery explosion ripped through it, an ear-shattering boom echoing through the streets. A large flame escaped from the top as the rear of the vehicle rocketed up, then crashed down heavily on the asphalt. The passersby on the street screamed in terror while darting to and fro. People ran and huddled for safety behind cars and other buses. Everyone in the Society's office building dived down and sheltered their heads.

Compared to the sound of the explosion, the scrambling outside seemed peaceful and controlled. Kitty was one of the first to look up and observe the surroundings. Her mouth hanging open in disbelief, she watched as shards of metal and rubber burned in the street. She teetered on the spot, unable to tear her eyes away from the burning bus and the mangled bodies spilling out of the vehicle.

From behind her, she heard yells as people tried to leave the building. Her senses jarred back to reality and she automatically made for the building's exit. She shouldered her way out of the office and onto the sidewalk. Kitty gasped as she looked around; all along the sidewalk were varying levels of injured people. Blood trickled down the concrete. Near her, a man cried out in pain while trying to pull out a large piece of metal from his leg. Kitty moved towards him to help, but then halted. She knew it would be a waste of valuable time to help the wounded; the paramedics and the police could handle that. Outside, a strong, freezing wind blew, tossing Kitty's flaxen hair higher and higher into the air. She glanced to where her car was parked down the street, but decided against driving; God knew what else would be blowing up within the next five minutes. Breaking into a brisk walk, Kitty clutched the papers in her fists as she flitted through the crowd on the sidewalk.

Firmly pushing people aside, the girl started moving faster, desperate to reach her home. Jogging now, the sounds of the chaos faded into the distance. Then, unexpectedly, another explosion ripped through the street behind Kitty. She broke into a run and didn't turn around to look. The tumult was enough to give her an idea of the scene. More people ran in the same direction as Kitty, jostling her as she went. A man shoved her aside, causing her to drop her purse and the reports she was carrying. She gave out a cry and turned to retrieve them, but they were trampled by the onslaught of people. Cursing under her breath, Kitty continued her flight.

Police cars and ambulances came down the street now, sirens wailing and lights flashing. A sense of hope filled her heart at the sight of police officers; here were fellow protectors of the peace, ready to handle any sort of situation. Her faith was quickly crushed, though, when she saw that some of the terrified citizens were being prevented from fleeing. One man tussled with a cop before the officer broke free from his grip and pushed the assailant down. As the man stumbled away, the police officer stood up, took out his gun, and fired. The bullet met the fleeing man's skull and he went down in a spray of blood. Soon, other officers followed suit. A row of police officers blocked off the street and shot into the oncoming crowd. Fresh cries filled the air as cold metal ripped through hot flesh. Many fell; some never got back up. Flanked on both sides by deadly forces, the populace scrambled, making an already chaotic situation much worse.

Damn. The Order got the police, too, Kitty thought to herself.

She turned into alleyway after alleyway to avoid the cops, but most of them lead to dead ends. For twenty minutes she skirted along, hiding and trying to get home. Finally, she spied an outlet just as an officer came striding down the road. She turned into the space between two looming grey buildings, slipping into the darkness. A tall fence obstructed her way and forced her to stop. She looked around the dark alleyway and noticed that the garbage cans and the dumpster created a natural step.

She took off her constricting heels and held them in one hand as she lifted herself onto a metal can, then moved to another one. Crouching, she placed her shoes on a large metal dumpster before heaving herself up. She replaced her shoes as she traversed the flat surface. Kitty breathed a sigh of thanks that the fence was flat, not spiked. She swung her right leg over the wooden plank while steadying herself with her hands. A loud, obnoxious bark nearly caused her to lose her balance; after regaining control, she looked down. Two large Dobermans snapped in a frenzied manner while clawing at the fence. She grimaced as she threw a shoe at them, hoping to either distract them or scare them off. But to no avail; there was no way to avoid them.

The girl sighed as she pulled out her M9 from inside her jacket pocket. She regretted what she had to do, but she was in too much of a rush to deal with the dogs now. Aiming at the animals, she made two clean headshots, silencing them in seconds. She swung both of her legs over, inhaled deeply, and pushed herself off of the fence. She somersaulted when she hit the ground then straightened herself out. She smiled to herself as she saw her house nearby; she had found a new emergency shortcut. She had a sneaking suspicion that she would be running for her life a lot more now.

The wind became stronger and moaned like a ghoul when Kitty made it to her front gate. Her hands were numb from the cold, causing her to keep slipping with the latch. Finally making her way into the yard, she strode over to the peeling red door and gripped the handle. She reached for her purse, but she remembered she had lost it along with her house keys. Fuming, she went over to the shrubs along the side of the house. Under a particularly bushy one, there was an old, unused rabbit hole hidden under dead foliage. Kitty stuck her hand inside and fished in the hollow until she could feel the small, cold key. She pulled it out, went over to the door, and let herself in. She carefully closed the door behind her and put the key in her pocket.

The girl went immediately to her room. It was oddly cold. Kitty went over to the ornate rug in the middle of the room and moved it aside. The doorway became visible and she unhooked the bronze latch. She gripped the top of the ladder and placed her foot on the fourth rung. Slowly, she went down and flipped a light switch. They flickered on and off for a few seconds before turning on, emitting a faint buzz in the process. Kitty turned from the ladder and inhaled sharply.

The small, dusty room was completely devoid of munitions.

Mouth agape, Kitty looked around. The once amply-stocked room hadn't a trace of weaponry. Everything had been taken: ammunition, handguns, machine guns, tactical knives, grenades, even the sole RPG she owned. The empty brown shelves stared back at Kitty like corpses. Searching for plausible answers, she clambered up the ladder. She looked about the room, hoping to find a sign of intrusion. She saw none. Kitty looked over to her desk and swore: her laptop had been taken as well.

Kitty strode over to a small nightstand that she had next to her bed and opened a drawer. She pulled out a large black flashlight-looking device. She walked back to the hatch. An eerie green light shone over everything, but Kitty grunted with dissatisfaction. She had not retrieved her wanted evidence: fingerprints. Going back down the ladder, she scanned the entire room, but found no trace of the thief. Kitty went back upstairs and continued her search, slowly roving the entire room. She found nothing.

Kitty moved towards to her ebony desk that was a few feet from her window. She was going to pass it by when she noticed her sheer white curtains fluttering slightly. Kitty frowned; she never opened her windows and there were no vents blowing. She was about to reach out to the curtains when she noticed a glittering trail on the floor. Crouching down, she saw that the gleaming particles led to under her bed. She went on her knees and looked under her bed. There, she found a pile of broken glass shoved to the side. Kitty blanched as she turned back to the windows. Holding her breath, she quickly drew away the white curtains. Fragments of glass fell from the window sill; the window was shattered and had a large hole in it. Where there was no damage, the characters *R 6 8* had been written in a carmine liquid which looked strikingly like blood.

Someone had broken in and taken Kitty's weapons. Whoever it was, they wanted the girl to know something and were going to make her look for the answers. Kitty closed her eyes and exhaled deeply; she had a feeling she had very little time to make sense of these three characters. She also had another feeling that the weaponry would be resurfacing much too soon.

IX

SURPRISES

Days passed before any other attacks were initiated. Kitty sat in her living room, the television set on the news. A young, blonde reporter was recapping the bombing in the city. The explosion alone had killed thirty people. The police massacre Kitty had witnessed was deemed an accident and the eighteen dead were mere casualties of an intense and confused situation. No one had claimed the attack yet, but Kitty, as well as the rest of the Society, was sure it was the doing of the Order.

She turned the TV off, tired of the repetition. She was more concerned about the possibility of the next attack and, more importantly, who had taken the weapons. Everyone in her department knew about the weapon vault in her house; it was a requirement for all Society members to know where weapon stores are in the state. However, many of the members lived far from her. The girl stood up and began to pace back and forth in the living room.

I haven't talked to anyone in weeks. Who had known my parents and I were out of the house? Kitty thought to herself, frowning. *How did they know where to find the weapon vault? And what does 'R 6 8' mean?*

She shook her head in confusion, unable to understand the situation. "I'm a recruiter, for Christ's sake, not a detective," she said aloud as she saw herself in the hallway mirror. She stared at her reflection, running her hand through her hair. She noticed the circles under her eyes; she hadn't slept properly ever since she'd come home, nor had she left the house.

She decided to call Chell to see how she was doing. Secretly, she also wanted to have a second opinion on her uncertain situation. She walked over to the house phone and dialed her friend's number. Kitty waited by the phone with the receiver at her ear. She could hear Chell's line ringing, but no one was picking up. The girl cursed aloud when the answering machine kicked in and hung up. The moment she put the receiver down it started to ring. Kitty swiped up the phone and smashed it against her face before the caller ID showed up.

"Hello? Chell?" she breathed, hoping to hear her friend's calming voice. "Uh, no. Kitty, this is Serene," the voice on the other line said. Kitty's heart fell with disappointment but she feigned interest for the sake of her other friend.

"Oh, hi, Serene! What's up?" Kitty asked.

"Is this line secure?" Serene asked quickly.

"Yes, yes, of course," Kitty replied nervously. "Why?"

"Um, have you checked the news lately?" Serene inquired.

"Yes, I've been watching the news all day. I'm getting pretty tired of it, too," Kitty said, giving a wary glance at the TV.

"No, not the tube. Have you read the paper?" Serene asked her, apprehension growing in her voice.

The blond girl frowned at the worried tone in her friend's voice. She pondered her recent hermit-like behavior and how much of the world had passed her by.

"Hold on a second, Serene," Kitty said nervously. She walked over to the front door and opened it, groaning at the sudden flash of sunlight. She bent down and picked up the stack of morning papers that she had failed to retrieve. Closing the door behind her, she grabbed the latest edition from the top and placed the older ones on a side table. She tucked the phone back into the crook of her neck and spoke into the receiver.

"Ok, Serene. What am I supposed to be looking at?" she said, glancing at the front page. A picture of the country's frazzled-looking president beamed up at her. She scanned the front page for anything that might pertain to her.

"Seventh page. Check the column at the far right corner," Serene said with almost bated breath.

Kitty looked to where her friend had indicated. A miniscule, unassuming news column was pushed out to the corner in fine print. Her eyes roved over the headline and let out a gasp of surprise.

"Good God," Kitty whispered into the receiver, her heart galloping in her chest. The words 'Joseph Harding Assassinated' rebounded against the walls of her brain. She stared goggle-eyed, unable to digest the news.

"Serene, you're sure this line is secure?" she asked breathlessly.

"Positive," came the reply.

"I can't believe it," Kitty said in a hushed tone. "What on Earth happened?"

"He was found dead this morning. His throat was slit open. The killer thought it would be fun to put a bullet in his head, too," Serene replied.

Kitty swallowed a nauseous wave that brewed in her throat. She certainly had no love for the man, but his horrific death just seemed too well-timed.

"Any indications as to who could have done it?" Kitty asked her friend, looking back at the news article.

"Well, no one has come forth and claimed the murder, but that's not a surprise seeing how sudden it is. Anyway, even if they did, the newspaper wouldn't release that information just yet. Wouldn't want to incite too much panic among the masses, y'know?" Serene answered slowly. Then, she dropped her voice to a hushed tone as she continued, "However, there is something odd about this murder. Something that makes it different from any other assassinations from the past."

Kitty shivered at the thought of a complication. The last thing she wanted to hear that there was another factor involved. "What do you mean, Serene?" she asked.

The other girl maintained her quieted tone as if in fear of being overheard. "I was there today, Kitty. I was at the building after the assassination. Whoever killed Harding must have been in the room with him, but there's no record of a meeting; the surveillance cameras in the lobby don't show anyone entering or leaving the office, nor did those in the area recall seeing anyone of questionable intent."

Kitty was silent for a moment. "That must mean that the assassin was inside the building before anyone else was. Is there any footage showing inside the office?"

Serene gave a rueful laugh. "Harding wouldn't permit it. He refused to have surveillance in his room, and no one had the authority or the guts to overrule him. But you know Harding; never in his wildest dreams would he have thought that he would have a future killer." Becoming more serious, she went on, "The only point of entry into that room other than the door would be the windows or the air vents. But both of them were untouched; in fact, the only indication that there was someone else in the room was Harding's dead body. However, that's not even the weirdest part. The bullet the killer used was one issued by the Society: the ones that have an indicator on them that can only be revealed under ultraviolet light."

"What's your point?"

"These bullets aren't issued to the public. Only members of the Society of Light can possess them. That means that whoever shot Harding was part of the Society."

Kitty's heart stopped and her blood ran cold. Pieces of an immense puzzle were starting to fall into place. "Or they stole it from a Society member," she said, closing her eyes and exhaling deeply.

"What?"

"Serene, a couple of days ago, someone broke into my house and stole all of my weapons."

"You're kidding me."

"I'm afraid not."

Serene was silent for a couple of seconds as she reflected on the news. "When did they have time to steal everything? You had a ton of stuff down there."

"Probably while I was at work. Also, the attack outside the building that day forced me to walk home, so they earned themselves some extra time."

"So that means whoever robbed you also knew that the buses outside your workplace was going to explode."

"Exactly."

"Jesus Christ, Kitty."

"Why are they targeting me? What did I ever do?" Kitty said, a feeling of anguish rushing through her.

"Now, now. They may not be necessarily targeting you solely. God only knows what the Order's reasoning is for anything."

"The Order?"

"Yes, of course. All of these attacks must be the work of the Order. Who else would pull off stunts like that? It's not like there's another terrorist group; if there was, we'd know about it."

"Hm."

"What's wrong, Kitty? You don't seem so sure," Serene asked.

Kitty shook her head before answering into the receiver. "I don't know, Serene. Something doesn't feel right. I have a feeling that this isn't the work of the Order. At least, not in the way that we're used to."

X

DECEPTION

After she had gotten off the phone with Serene, Kitty went to her personal library to find the meaning of 'R 6 8'. After two hours of searching, she found nothing. Cursing, she decided to break free of her self-created confinement and leave the house. She ran upstairs and quickly took a warm shower, wishing she could wash away the traumatic events that had occurred. She changed into a pair of blue jeans and a green belted tunic. Kitty arranged her golden hair into a messy bun and slipped a black headband over the front. She grabbed a pair of comfortable flats from her closet, keeping in mind that she may have to flee at any given moment. She also grabbed a jacket; she could see the wind whipping through the barren branches of the trees. Before she left, she checked all of the windows and doors, making sure they were locked. Her eyes swept across the room, looking for anything that she might not want to be exposed. She was relieved that her broken bedroom window could not be easily seen from the outside; she didn't want a random passerby to become too curious. Satisfied that there was nothing for a thief to take, Kitty grabbed her purse and headed out the door, locking it behind her.

Her car was still parked by the Society building, so she decided to walk down to it. "Perhaps I'll stop by the library on my way to my car to get a lead on what 'R 6 8' could possibly mean. Maybe get a muffin while I'm at it," Kitty said to herself, clutching her bag slightly tighter as she proceeded down the sidewalk. It was extremely quiet in the neighborhood; many of the residents had either moved or stayed secluded within their homes. Kitty didn't blame them, either. After the bombing in the city, many people had feared for their lives.

Kitty hated it all: the fear, the constant uncertainty, the endless chances of dying. She hated living in a world that always seemed to hold its breath. As she walked down the long deserted sidewalk, she remembered what life was like when she was a girl. The Crisis had already existed, but it wasn't as bad. At least, in her childish innocence, it didn't seem so. There weren't as many empty houses, not as many loved ones dying, and not as much fear riddling the populace. There were always tales of assassinations and bombings in other countries but it didn't quite click with everyone; they didn't seem to understand the seriousness of the situation. But the moment the Order's gaze fell onto the States, everything changed.

She crossed out from her development to an area filled with small shops and places of entertainment. She stopped in a small, dusty café and ordered a blueberry muffin with coffee. As she sat by the window seat waiting for her food, she watched the other people going about their daily business.

"They don't smile at each other anymore. They just keep their heads down and stare at the ground." Kitty said to her portly waiter, indicating to the people outside.

"Aye, lass. But, who can blame them? Their only interest is gettin' to where they're goin' without getting blown to bits in the next five minutes," he replied, watching a balding businessman that had broken into a slow jog. "People are just scared, is all. Nothin' against no one; they're just tryin' to get home alive."

With that, he placed her food down and moved away. Kitty dumped two packets of sugar into her coffee and poured in some cream. Staring blankly at the world outside, she tried again to make sense of the odd writings on her window. What 'R 6 8' could mean, she had no idea. Kitty chuckled at the fact that she was going to the library for answers; what she needed was a cryptographer.

She finished her snack quickly in order to be on her way. After she paid, Kitty left the café and headed towards the library. She jogged up the cracked stone steps that had grayed with age. Before she had reached the door, a familiar face emerged from the great stone building.

"Axel!" Kitty cried, smiling at the sight of her old friend. She ran and embraced him before stepping back to see how he had changed. He was tanner than she remembered. He was clad in a pair of grey jeans and his agile but muscular body was defined by his graphite long-sleeved shirt. His onyx hair swayed in the breeze, momentarily uncovering his jewel-bright eyes. He was taller and even more handsome than she remembered, but she was immediately struck by an odd air that seemed to hover around him.

"Hello, Kitty. I haven't seen you in an extremely long time," he replied with a smile. "What have you been up to lately?"

"Bah, you know, stuff for the Society. It's been crazy with all of the bombings and attacks," Kitty said grimly, thinking back to the day she was forced to flee her workplace.

"Ah, yes. I can only imagine the headaches you have to take on. I truly pity you and all those in your line of work," he said lightly. Kitty raised an eyebrow. There was something in his tone that was strange but at the same time very familiar. However, she could not place it. Unwilling to dampen the moment, she changed the subject.

"So, what have you been doing with yourself lately?" she asked him. Before he could answer, Kitty peered at the worn leather-bound book that he had in hand. The title gleamed up at her in gold lettering.

"The Bible?" Kitty asked with mild interest. "I thought you were an atheist, Axel."

He gave a small smile. "Oh, I am. I still don't believe in God or any of the other phantoms that people have created. Nor do I believe in most of the things that their books dictate. However, there are still some things in here that I can't fully disagree with." He then tilted his head slightly and his smile widened. His peacock-blue eyes gleamed with a knowing, mischievous twinkle. Again, the same mysterious air became apparent to Kitty before he spoke. "But you know what my favorite book in the Bible is? Revelation. It has taught me some things. Great things," he said with an almost trance-like voice. "You should read it; it will open your eyes."

"Open my eyes to what?" Kitty asked, frowning, unable to overlook the change in her friend's behavior.

He replied, "You'll see soon enough, Kitty. But I must be on my way. It was lovely talking to you." With a small wave of his hand, Axel turned away from his friend, a slightly triumphant smirk plastered on his face.

Kitty stared after the boy and watched as he crossed the street and walked towards a cardinal red convertible. Their conversation echoed in her mind as she tried to make sense of its strangeness. She reached towards the handle, still keeping an eye on Axel's car as he drove away. As he went out of sight, the girl suddenly thought of who Axel had reminded her of: Joseph Harding. He had that same look on his face that the late executive had: a look of knowing conceit. But there was something else, she thought to herself. Something evil about him.

Kitty shook her head and walked into the vast library. Great chandeliers hung overhead, their melting tapers casting a soft, yellowish glow in the main area. Up ahead, a slight, elderly woman sat reading at the check-out desk, her rimless glasses resting precariously on the tip of her nose. Hearing Kitty's footsteps, she looked up and smiled at the girl.

"Can I help you find something, dear?" she asked sweetly.

Kitty tried to imagine where she could possibly find answers to the blood message, then replied, "I need to find books on codes, abbreviations, and cryptology."

The librarian raised an eyebrow but made no comment on the girl's demands. Instead, she pointed in the direction which Kitty needed to go. The girl thanked the woman and headed towards the shelves in the lonely back corner of the library. She arrived to a section filled with old books that seemed to see little use. Her heart sank as she surveyed the endless number of titles. Kitty craned her neck to glance at the librarian, but she was nowhere in sight. Dismissing the woman as useless, Kitty sighed and grabbed a thick book that sat on the shelf in front of her. Dust emerged from the shelf as she examined the book's cover. It was a history of code usage during wars of old. Frowning, Kitty picked up a book farther along the shelf and peered at the title; it too was not relevant to her situation. She sighed again.

Time went by as she searched for some hint concerning her troubling message, but with little success. The few people who passed through the secluded section glanced at Kitty questioningly as she got down on her hands and knees to examine the texts on the lower levels. Another hour passed before Kitty straightened up from her hunched-over position and looked around. On the far wall of the library, there was a table covered in a purple silken fabric and stacked with different religious texts. Sunlight from the window above it shone down and the books' gilded pages glittered across the aisle. Kitty thought back to Axel and his strange interest with the book of Revelation. Suddenly, Kitty's eyes grew wide as realization dawned on her.

"R 6 8. Revelation, Chapter 6 verse 8," Kitty mumbled to herself as she stood and walked over to the table. She solemnly picked up a large, leather-bound Bible and slowly opened its burgundy cover. She flipped all the way to the back and scanned the pages for the section she was looking for. As Kitty read the verse, her eyes grew wide and her heart started to pound in her chest.

"And I looked, and behold a pale horse: and the name that sat on him was Death, and Hell followed with him," she said breathlessly. Her eyes traveled to a small piece of paper that had been taped over the rest of the verse. With trembling fingers, she removed the small note and opened it. She knew it was addressed to her. She paled as she read the thickly scribbled message:

WE ARE COMING.

The girl put her hand to her chest, trying to steady her frenzied heart. Swallowing, she stowed the note in her pocket and set the Bible back down onto the table. Trying not to raise any suspicion, Kitty clutched onto her bag and stoically walked to the front. As she approached the door, the librarian looked up at her and asked, "Did you find what you were looking for, dear?"

Kitty forced a smile and nodded before she walked out of the library. Once out in the open, she inhaled deeply to clear the frightened feeling that stuck in her throat. She looked up at the sky. The sun was struggling to pierce through the grey fog that hung over the land. Around her, people were bustling about their business, but their jaws were set and their eyes were misted, incapable of humor or light. Kitty frowned; the entire surrounding seemed alien to her. Her senses were muted; the entire landscape was dull. For the first time, she saw the bleakness of her world.

She, like everyone else, had gone through her life without realizing the ominous veil of despair that clung to the city. But her eyes were now open; at least, they were more open than those around her.

"Something terrible is going to happen. I can feel it," Kitty said aloud as she surveyed the scene once more. She needed to talk to Chell; she knew that she could always find some sanity from her. Spotting a comfortable-looking bench, the girl sat down and brought out her cell phone. With shaking fingers, she selected Chell's name from the contacts list and pressed 'Call.'

****

Chell watched the phone earnestly, waiting for it to spark to life. Her eyes were fixed on the device. When it did ring, she smiled; she had been anticipating this call all day. Chell waited for it to sound three times before answering it.

"Hello?" she asked, pretending as though she didn't know who was calling.

"Chell?" a worried, stressed voice inquired on the other line.

"Oh, hello, Kitty," Chell answered, picking up a beige teddy bear from her bed and pressing it against her cheek.

"Chell, is this line secure? Are you alone?" Kitty half-whispered.

"Mhm," Chell answered. She leaned against the doorway frame. The house was empty, save her; her mother and grandmother had already been taken to the Sanctuary. "What's up?"

"Chell, we've got a problem. A lot of problems. I-I don't know where to start," Kitty stammered.

The raven-haired girl smiled grimly. "Why don't you start from the beginning?"

There was a brief silence on the other end; Chell assumed that Kitty recognized the dialogue from their previous conversations. Then, she started.

"Well, everything started after my visit with Joseph Harding."

"Oh, you never told me about that. How did your meeting go?" Chell asked, her cheeks heating slightly.

"Well, I went there trying to find out why the bombings took place. He wouldn't tell me anything. Before I left the building, two buses outside blew up. It killed about two dozen people. I didn't bother getting my car so I had to run home. When I finally got there, I found out that someone had broken into my home and stolen all of my weapons from the vault."

Kitty paused for a breath, expecting her friend to ask her to repeat some of the information. However, Chell only told her to proceed with her story.

"Ok. After I found out that the weapons were gone, I saw a message that someone had written in blood. It was 'R 6 8'. Then, today I found out that Joseph Harding had been assassinated. They still have no clue who did it, but I have a theory."

"And that theory is?" Chell asked.

"Whoever killed Harding was a Society agent. And a pretty damn good one, at that. They killed Harding with Society-issued bullets, making it almost impossible to trace. The gun was never found."

"Continue," Chell ordered.

"I also have another theory. One about Axel," Kitty sighed.

Chell frowned slightly. She knew what Kitty was going to say, but she didn't think it would come out so soon.

"Chell, I think that Axel is working against us. I think he is working for the Order," she said. "I met him outside of the library. He seemed...strange. There was definitely something different about him. Anyway, he was carrying a Bible on his way out, and he told me to read the Book of Revelation. That it would 'open my eyes'. After he left, I went inside the library. It finally hit me what 'R 6 8' meant: Revelation, chapter six, verse eight. In the library there was a table with Bibles on it. I opened one and looked for that verse. It talked about Hell in the form of a horse and its rider, Death, wreaking havoc on earth. And," Kitty inhaled slowly, "there was a message taped into that book. It said 'we are coming' in big bolded lettering. They had meant for me to find it, Chell. They wanted me to know. They are going to attack."

"Anything else?" Chell asked, picking up a nail file and rounding out the edge of her nail.

"Chell, aren't you the least bit perturbed by any of this?" Kitty asked in bewilderment.

"Not really. "

"My theory on Axel doesn't surprise you at all?"

"Nope. I already knew about that."

"What?!?"

"Kitty, Axel went over to the Order long ago."

"And you said nothing about it?" Kitty yelled on the other line.

"Of course not. Why would I expose him?"

"Did you ever consider your duty to the Society, Chell?" Kitty asked, trying to keep her voice level.

Chell gave a short, dry laugh. "Did *I* consider my duty? You bet I did! I considered it as long as the Society kept its duty to me! But that didn't happen, now, did it?"

"What do you mean, 'the Society didn't keep its duty?' "

Chell's temper suddenly flared. "What about the whole 'your family will be kept safe' thing, huh? What about the whole 'they won't get hurt' part?"

"Chell, that wasn't the Society's fault."

"Oh, please, Kitty, don't give me that. They told me that it was the Society who dropped the bomb the day they hauled my dead family away! They specifically told me that those villains were the ones who dropped it! So don't you tell me that it wasn't the Society's fault!"

Kitty said nothing; Chell knew that she wouldn't. After all, what was there to say? Then, Kitty piped up.

"Chell, I'm sorry. I understand that you're hurt by all this. Believe me, I'm hurt, too. But let me assure you, the Society is a benign institution; we fight for good, not evil. Always remember that."

"Oh, I know, Kitty, I know," Chell replied blankly. "Hey, listen, I wanna talk to you about some things. I'd like to see you in person. How 'bout I pick you up in thirty minutes and we can talk in the car and get some coffee?" she asked.

Kitty smiled, surprised but thankful that her friend had returned back to normal. "That sounds great, Chell. I'll be waiting for you, ok?"

"Alright, sounds good. Thanks, Kitty. I'll see you soon," Chell said cheerfully. The moment she hung up, her face fell from its gleaming smile to a grim scowl.

"Benign institution. Right," she muttered under her breath as she threw her cell phone on her bed. She grabbed her jacket and walked out of her room, turning to a white door. She opened it and a dim light flickered on, revealing a flight of wooden steps. Chell went down into the basement and walked over to a padlocked cabinet with frosted glass that was mounted on the wall. Above the cabinet was written, 'If the need arises'. *The need has certainly arisen*, thought Chell. She set the combination for the lock and opened the door. Inside was a black cell phone with a glossy outer shell; another secured phone, but not one issued by the Society. She picked it up and punched in a phone number.

"Yes, C?" a male voice answered.

"It's time. Inform the initiation department that Operation Phoenix must start as soon as possible," Chell said.

"Will do."

"Oh, and when you're done with that, I need you to come over. Operation Vendetta is starting today. Don't use your car; pick me up in the sedan. Bring all of the necessary supplies."

"Are you sure you want to do this?"

"Sure as I'll ever be."

"Alright. I'll see you soon."

Chell hung up and went back upstairs. She walked over to the living room and leaned in the frame of the door. In a corner, a small table was placed there with pictures of her father and brother. The photos were surrounded by flower petals and incense. Chell walked over to the memorial and picked up a lighter that was off to the side. She ignited a rod of incense, inhaling the sweet perfumed smoke that rose from it. The girl glanced down lovingly at the pictures before her, stroking the glass of her brother's portrait. *He looks so innocent*, Chell thought to herself. Her eyes roved to her father's face, proud and full of life. Memories of summers spent boating by the lake, birthday cakes being cut, and hugs being shared flooded her mind. She squeezed her eyes shut, letting the tears roll down her face.

Chell stood there for minutes before drying her eyes. She turned away as she heard the sound of a car pulling up into her driveway. She hurried out of the living room and put her jacket on. She stopped and held her breath before she opened the door. Now, everything would fall into place. It was finally time.

XI

RECKONING

About two hours away in the town of Coronus, Pennsylvania, Ian Hamilton was outside raking leaves from the front yard. He crammed the dry leaves into a tall pile at the base of an enormous oak tree. Finally satisfied with it, the boy smiled at his work and leaned against the handle of the rake. He eyed an unfinished section of the yard wearily before trudging in that direction. No sooner had he stooped over the rake when he heard a loud battle cry followed by an immense crunch. Ian whirled around to see his twin brother buried waist deep in a pile of sere foliage; the same pile that Ian had just raked.

"No! Look what you've done!" Ian yelled in dismay as Jared stood up beaming.

"My apologies, dear brother! I couldn't resist the temptation!" Jared exclaimed, shaking crinkly leaves from his beach-blonde hair.

Ian threw the rake at his brother, who deftly caught it.

"Not funny. You're going to clean that up." Ian said, thrusting his chin in the direction of the scattered leaves.

"What! Oh, come now! You know I can't rake!" Jared protested. He began backing away from his brother, but he tripped on a sturdy tree branch, sending him falling into a fresh pile of leaves. He sat up, blowing decaying plant matter out of his mouth. Ian giggled uncontrollably at his brother's appearance; Jared started to laugh as well. Ian thrust his hand out for Jared to grab, then pulled the other boy up. The sound of approaching planes broke their fraternal bonding moment as the pair looked up at the sky. Up above, they could see a small squadron of planes soar ominously overhead. Small objects began dropping from the planes and hurtling down to the town.

"What on earth are they-OH MY GOD JARED RUN!"

Ian grabbed his brother's arm and jerked him towards the house, but one of the plane's packets collided with their roof. It exploded and the entire house was consumed by a wave of fire and napalm. The planes unleashed a barrage of explosions that quickly overtook the town. From below, the impact of bombs and the screams of the citizens rose high above the smoke and destruction that had swiftly erupted. People ran from their homes. The stench of burning wood and charred flesh filled the noses of the fleeing and the hellish glow of the fires continued to swell. The feeble flight was soon destroyed as the last of the bombs met their marks.

Up above, the squadron leader spoke into the radio.

"Mission was successful, Commander. Coronus is in flames. Standing by for the next attack."

****

Chell exited her home and locked the door. Outside, a sleek, black sedan with tinted windows was waiting for her. Chell strolled over to it and went inside. The person who had been sitting in the driver's seat nodded to her and went around to the back. She brought the car out of its parked stage and slammed her foot on the gas.

Later, she arrived at the library. She raised her hand, giving a signal to the person in the back. She glanced down and saw Kitty sitting nervously on a bench. Then, she stepped out of the car. She softened her expression as she went up the steps, trying not to look suspicious. Kitty heard her approach and quickly got up. She flew out towards Chell and engulfed her in a hug.

"You don't know how happy I am to see you," Kitty said breathlessly, scrutinizing her friend's every detail. "I was afraid you wouldn't show!"

Chell just smiled, and directed her friend to her car.

"New car, huh? Since when were you into tinted windows?" Kitty asked. Chell tensed slightly, but then dismissed Kitty's comment as purely conversational.

"Ever since the attack, actually," Chell replied. "It seemed like everyone knew what had happened. I hated the sympathy looks I would get every time I went into town. They all seemed to know who I was, even though I had no clue who they are. It was nice at first, but then it just got irritating."

At this, Kitty said nothing but proceeded to the passenger side of the car. She entered and sat down in the grey leather seat, admiring the modern interior.

"Comfortable!" Kitty exclaimed as Chell closed her door. The blonde girl began digging into her purse for her makeup. Seeing an opportunity, Chell quickly locked the door and made a discreet hand motion. Kitty found what she was looking for and pulled down the visor, but suddenly, a man reached out with gloved hands from behind. He grabbed Kitty's slender throat in one hand and smashed a saturated cloth against her nose and mouth with the other. Kitty's first instinct was to scream but she was too busy gasping for breath. She desperately clawed at the assailant's hands, but to no avail; he only made his grip tighter. Slowly, she could feel the world spinning before her as the drugging agent began to set in; the interior of the car becoming a grey blur. Her eyes sluggishly rolled to look at Chell, but the friend's expression was blurred out. Before she could determine the nature of the attack, Kitty slumped into unconsciousness.

"Good. Nicely done," Chell said as she put on a pair of purple silk gloves. "The less evidence, the better."

"Poor girl. She is in for one *hell* of a surprise when she gets to the pit," the assailant said, leaning back into the seat with a satisfied smirk on his face.

"That's exactly what I intend."

****

Kitty's eyes slid open and adjusted to the light that shone down on her. She craned her neck slowly, trying to determine where she was. The room was small and dark, with the intense light that beamed on her being the only source of illumination. It was furnished with the most bizarre assortment of items; there was a table filled with various instruments, a television, oil barrels, multiple hay bales and the chair that Kitty was strapped in. She looked down at her seat. The chair was shaped like those found in a dental office, but was much less comfortable. Kitty then realized that her arms and legs were strapped to the seat with thick leather belts. Eyes wide, she started struggling violently against her restraints, but it only cut into her skin more and more.

"I would advise you not to do that."

Kitty's head spun to the direction of the voice. Standing by a hidden doorway was Axel. He looked the same as when the girl had met him outside the library, but the smirk of triumph on his face could not be overlooked. Kitty realized that this was the person who had drugged her.

"You! Where on Earth am I? What did you do to Chell?" Kitty yelled at the boy, glaring at him.

"One thing at a time, comrade. First, let's make sure you won't be going anywhere," Axel said with a smile, walking over to the chair. He placed his hand on the girl's bonds and tightened the strap. "To answer your first accusation, yes, it is me. However, I'm not alone in this, as you may have already figured out. As to where you are, I won't bother telling you for it matters little at this point. And as for the current location of our friend Chell..."

"She's right here."

The door opened and closed again. From the shadows emerged Chell, who smiled sweetly at Kitty. She drifted up to Axel's side, who subsequently snaked his strong arm around her waist.

"You poor, confused girl," Chell said with mock sympathy as Kitty stared at the pair.

"Chell...what is going on?" Kitty asked, her voice small and choked with tears.

Chell sighed and began to pace back and forth in front of the chair before she began.

"Do you remember what you had told me in my backyard? When you were trying to get me to join the Society?" Chell asked her calmly, glancing at her with her head tilted.

"...No," Kitty responded, unsure of where her captor was going with the conversation.

"Of course not," Chell said, rolling her eyes. "You had told me that by joining the Society of Light, my family would receive protection from whatever was to come. However, that obviously didn't happen."

"Chell, that was all a--"

"Let me finish. The Society of Light killed my father and my brother. They also torched my house. They left my mother a recluse and the remainder of my family in emotional, psychological, and financial disarray. Naturally, I was pissed. I was *beyond* pissed. I knew I had to take action, but at first I was confused what exactly I'd do. Yes, a terrorist attack was all fun and everything, but I needed to address the problem at hand. Then it came to me. Since I was already in the Society of Light, I knew who would have been in command of the attack that killed my family."

There was a pause as Chell waited for Kitty to pick up on what she was saying. Kitty stared blankly at her for a few moments, trying to understand. But then, it hit her.

"...Oh, my God, Chell," Kitty said, eyes growing wide.

"Yes, Kitty, dear. I decided to pay Mr. Joseph Harding a little visit. I'll even show you how that went. I made a little video of it just for you." With that, she pulled a small remote out of her pocket and aimed it at the blank TV screen across the room. It turned on and started playing a video. Onscreen, it showed the outside world. It was dark, but the sounds of the city could still be heard. Kitty assumed that the cameraperson was Chell. The camera, most likely built into one of her accessories, was engaged in a slow but continuous ascent. Chell looked up and Kitty was able to see that the black mass in front of the camera was the sleek glass side of a building. It took Kitty a while to realize that it was her workplace.

"You scaled a forty-two story building," Kitty said flatly as she continued watching the screen.

"It's not that hard if you've got the right equipment and enough stamina. The key thing is not to let go," Chell replied. She skipped parts of the movie. It continued playing and showed a view of the roof. In the video, Chell then slipped into large air duct. It became hard to see and Kitty could barely make out the sides of the air vent. After a few minutes, however, light came streaming in from a grill; Chell had reached her destination. A loud metallic thud indicated that the assassin had more than just a camera with her. Chell looked towards a dark duffel bag and leaned in closer so the camera could capture the contents. Inside she could see wrenches, knives, and handguns of all sorts. Chell took out a massive drill and began unscrewing the bolts on the grill, but didn't remove it. Chell fast-forwarded the movie before pausing it.

"I waited for him," Chell told Kitty, shifting her weight and crossing her arms. "Like a tiger waits for its prey. I knew that he came earlier than anyone else in the building; my informants were able to confirm this for me. Sure enough, at five o'clock in the morning, Joseph Harding came sweeping into his office with coffee in one hand and a briefcase in the other. The rest of the employees came to work later on. The business day started." She zoned off while staring at the screen, an expression of anger plastered on her face. "I wanted to kill him so badly, but I knew that I would have to wait. They couldn't find him dead first thing in the morning; they would have blamed the cleaning ladies or some other poor soul if that had happened. But that's not what I wanted. I didn't want them to think they'd "gotten" someone. No, he had to see other people throughout the day before dying. That would make it *really* confusing. Then they'd start to feel afraid, because they truly wouldn't know who could have done it."

Chell played the rest of the movie. It showed her stationary, watching Harding's every move. Although she could hear the buzz of the lobby outside, no one came to visit him. He walked back and forth across the office, deep in thought. The girl was as silent and stiff as a corpse; her camera didn't even pick up her breathing. Suddenly, Chell sensed an arising opportunity and silently moved the grill back. Harding continued to pace around in his room, before coming to a halt in front of a large portrait of himself on the far right wall. Chell dropped down soundlessly and took off the camera. She set it down on a chest of drawers behind her; the recording showed her decked in a black, wet-looking catsuit with her hair under a skullcap. Harding was too absorbed in admiring his own image to hear her approach.

Inaudibly, Chell took a knife from her hip, ran up behind him and slammed her lithe body against his. She reached towards his mouth and stifled his yell before bringing the blade to his throat. In a lightning move, she made a deep, long gash across his neck. Blood cascaded from the wound as he reached up to his throat. Beads of crimson liquid trickled from between Chell's gloved fingers. Harding's knees buckled and the final convulsions of death took hold of him. Chell lowered him to the ground. He looked helplessly at Chell but his voice was drowned out. Then, his eyes rolled up into his skull and his writhing slowly ceased. A pool of blood formed around Harding as his corpse lay sprawled on the carpet. Chell straddled Harding's body and pulled out a gun. She gently rested it between his eyes and pulled the trigger once, sending a jerk throughout the dead body. With a triumphant air, the girl slowly stood up and stretched. She took one final glance at the pathetic man before looking away.

Chell replaced her weapons and walked towards the camera. She picked it up and put it back on its original perch. She unwrapped a cord from around her waist; it had a sophisticated hooking device at the end of it. Swiftly, Chell swung the rope and launched the end of it up into the air vent from which she came. The small but powerful disk on the end immediately reacted to the metal vents and activated its puissant suction cup. The girl tugged on the line to make sure it was secure before slinking back up to the vent. Once there, the assassin replaced the grill, tightening the bolts with all of her might. The video then stopped.

"You silenced the gun," Kitty said with distaste.

"Of course. Even in that chaotic mess they call a department, unchecked gun shots would still be heard." She paused before continuing. "He had no clue I was there. I made sure I didn't give him any warning. Anything that would involve noise I handled before he arrived. I tested the grill a couple of times to see how much noise it would make. I went up and down that rope a thousand times to see how much time I would have and how stealthy I could be. I had people on the inside deactivate security systems, reroute the janitors, the whole nine yards. All of this I did to avoid detection, because that was the last thing I wanted. Sudden and shocking, just like Jack's and Dad's deaths."

"Are you happy now, you sick monster? The person who directed that operation is dead. Are you satisfied?" Kitty spat at her, feelings of anger and grief mingling inside of her.

"Not yet. There's someone else who needs to be dealt with; the hellhag who talked me into joining that stupid Society. The one who dragged me into this whole mess."

"Wait, WHAT?"

Chell nodded to Axel, who gleefully moved over to the instrument-laden table. He picked up a syringe and stuck the needle into a small jar. Pulling backwards, a purple liquid flooded the vial. Axel flicked the side of the syringe with intent.

"You may not realize it now, Kitty, but you are the reason all of this started. You see, after the attack, I confronted my mother about what exactly my dad did. Turns out he was also part of the Society. He was an aeronautical engineer, working and designing the very planes that would eventually kill him. He was suspicious from the very beginning and his suspicions were confirmed when he traveled overseas. He saw what Society members allowed and practiced over in places where they thought no one could touch them: inhumane detention, raping of prisoners, experimental mutations, everything. After my dream, my father started making some bold statements. You may not have known, but the Society was quite keen on experimenting on me to see what else my brain can produce for them. It wouldn't have been legal without my consent, but that didn't bother them. It upset my father, though. He was totally against the fact that the Society was considering doing experiments because of my dream. Along with that, he began exposing all the crazy practices that the Society was trying. Naturally, they didn't like that someone was challenging them, especially because that person could easily start a rebellion since that person's daughter had insight about the Order of Shadows. Thus, they decided to...eliminate the threat."

She paused before continuing. "However, I guess I should thank you. Because of you, I realized how screwed up this world truly is. I was able to see that there can be no such thing as the 'good guy' in the current system. The ones that you thought would help you the most are just as evil as those you're trying to defeat."

"Tell me about it," Kitty said through clenched teeth as she glared at her former friend. Chell ignored her and continued.

"I realized that there needs to be a new world order; one without two-faced idiots running the show like they're gods. The Ordumbra showed me this. With the training I got from the Society and my own convictions, I was able to outperform everyone else. In fact, I grasped their mission so well that I was skyrocketed in my position in no time. They let me handle the good stuff."

"Good stuff?" Kitty asked, eyebrow raised.

"Yeah, good stuff. Who do you think detonated the buses outside of your workplace?" She switched the TV to a news channel which was covering the destruction of Coronus. Kitty's mouth dropped open.

"I initiated that attack before I picked you up. Because of me, that entire city has been decimated. And there's more coming." Chell's breath came faster and her eyes grew wider. An almost childlike excitement mounted inside of her. "Today, I'm bringing out the big guns. The killing machines are going to get their turn. Sadly, your death will not be by their hands." With that, Chell moved towards the table and dragged it closer to Kitty. The blond girl could see that it was covered with chemicals and weapons. She finally realized what Chell planned to do with her.

"Chell, please. I'm sorry! I didn't mean to cause any harm!" Kitty pleaded as she twisted against her bonds. She thrashed back and forth but was unable to set herself free.

"Well, you did! You DID cause harm! Now you're going to pay for it!" Chell bellowed at her, grabbing a whip from the table. Kitty yelped as Axel dug the needle into her arm and injected her with the violet liquid.

"That will make you feel pain like you've never felt before. Every injury I inflict, you'll feel it ten times over," Chell said wickedly, unfurling the whip. She then snapped her wrist and cracked the whip against Kitty's face. A red burn mark glowed angrily as Kitty began to scream.

"You think that hurts?" Chell yelled, cracking the whip at her several times. Over and over again, the leather cord cut into Kitty's skin. Little flecks of blood spotted her face and flew off the whip. Kitty's frenzied screams were amplified in the small room. Axel merely looked on with marked boredom.

After a few minutes, Chell stopped and threw the whip on the ground while Kitty broke into hysterical sobs. Axel brought another syringe and injected Kitty. "This is to make sure you don't faint," he said. Chell walked over to the table and picked up a series of sharp knives. Kitty's eyes grew wide in fear as she guessed the intent. With a smile, Chell stuck a knife in the girl's right thigh, just shy of her femoral artery. Kitty screamed again. Chell grabbed a second knife and plunged it into Kitty's left knee, sending spasms through the girl's body. With impressive speed, Chell dug another into her right shoulder. Blood flowed from the wounds like water and spilled onto the floor in rivers. Pain flooded through Kitty as she wailed. Chell laughed at the girl's misery, recalling every detail of her brother's mangled face. It was twisted in the same expression of pain as Kitty's.

"And for the final blow," Chell said before she rammed the last knife into Kitty's stomach. A strawberry ocean pooled about the girl's feet, but Kitty wasn't dead yet. She screamed with all of her might until her throat was hoarse and coated with blood.

Chell straightened out and admired her handiwork. Axel, however, consulted his wristwatch.

"Chell, we don't have much time. We need to leave soon," he said.

She did not hear him. Chell's attention was fixed on the gasping girl in front of her. Her eyes were open wide and a fiery madness burned within them.

"You little fool. So concerned, so *trusting*. Wanting to make the world safe for democracy and fairness. Wanting to make a *difference*. And where did that get you?" Chell asked as she leaned in close to Kitty. "Strapped to a chair with your guts in your lap. Alone and forgotten."

Kitty slowly picked her head up to look at Chell, mustering strength to express her disgust. She spat blood into Chell's face and croaked, "Go to hell."

Chell laughed wildly as she placed her hand on the knife in Kitty's stomach. With the other hand, she swiftly grabbed Kitty's throat and choked her. "Oh, I intend to. But before I go, I would see my destiny fulfilled. I would see this noble war play out. And even if this all ends in death and madness, I would see this world full of hypocrites razed to the ground." With that, she pushed the knife deeper into Kitty. The girl's screams continued on. Chell laughed aloud with sickening delight.

"CHELL!" Axel yelled from behind.

Chell's laughter stopped abruptly as her spell of madness left her. She wavered as reality slowly crept back to her. She straightened up and looked to Axel blankly before nodding and walking towards him.

Axel dragged over a large barrel from the corner. Chell followed and stooped down. With her accomplice, she lifted the barrel up and spilled the contents all over Kitty. Jet oil mingled with her blood as she spit it out of her mouth. It coated the floor and ran towards a small drain on the floor.

From the corner, the pair brought forth bales of hay. The gutted girl watched in anguish as bundles of dried grass were placed around her in a semicircle. The two assailants stood close to the exit and gazed at Kitty.

"Well, it's been nice, Kitty, dear. But the fun's got to end sometime, right?" Chell said airily. "However, we wanted to make this memorable for you, so Axel and I have decided to give you a proper farewell. You will be leaving this world in a similar manner as my father and brother did." With that, Axel took a lighter and a small bundle of hay in his hand. "Arrivederci, Katarina. Would love to stay and watch, but we've got to dash," Axel said. He lit the bundle on fire and thrust it at the girl. Then, both Axel and Chell ran out of the room. They sprinted into the hallway and out of the building into the sunlight. Inside, Kitty writhed in her chair and screamed aloud as her flesh seared. Her golden locks, now dyed red and black, burst into flames. The intense pain drove her insane, but the fast-acting poisons implanted in her refused to let her succumb immediately. The agonizing seconds felt like hours, but eventually, Kitty, as well as her shrieks, was completely consumed by the flames.

Outside, Axel and Chell clambered up a hill where their car was parked and watched the silent, grey building from afar.

"How do we know she's dead?" Axel asked her as he leaned back on the car.

"That room will be nothing more than a charred shell by the time anyone finds her," Chell replied. "Does that answer your question?"

Axel turned to her and looped his arms around her waist. She placed her slender arms around his shoulders and gazed at him.

"You, my dear, are a marvel," Axel cooed.

"I do what I can," she replied, drawing him closer and tightening her grip.

"And you do it well," he said. He tilted her head and enveloped her lips in a deep kiss. She kissed him back before transitioning to a tight embrace.

"Oh God, I love you," she whispered.

Axel placed his forehead against hers and looked into her eyes. "And I love you. Once this is all over, we'll forge this new world together. No one can stop us," he replied, then started to kiss her again. They stood fixed on the spot before they separated, smiling lovingly at one another.

"Come. There's work to be done," Chell said, opening the car door. Axel consented and went over to the passenger side. After he had gotten in, Chell took off. She smiled to herself. She was finally going to play with the instruments foretold in her dream, and she was going to play dirty.

XII

ASCENSION

Chell raced down the fairly empty highway as the sun struggled to penetrate the clouds. She said nothing as the surrounding area became a blur. Meanwhile, Axel watched in slight horror as the dashed white road line blended together. They continued driving as green overhead signs started to become visible. Axel moved up in his seat as he squinted at one pointing straight ahead.

"Chell, why are we going to the city? And where *are* we--"

He was cut short as Chell suddenly swerved to the right. She cut in front of a minivan and drove across occupied lanes to get to an exit; honks and the sound of breaking glass followed behind her.

"What the hell was that about?" Axel asked incredulously as a small smile crept onto Chell's face.

"For fun," came her reply. Axel stared at her for a little while longer before facing the front, a smile playing on his lips as well.

"We're going to the Sanctuary," Chell remarked a few minutes afterwards. "Ever been there?"

"No, actually. They took my parents there, but I never went myself. You?" Axel answered.

"A couple of times. It's one hell of a place. Never seen anything quite like it," said Chell.

As they continued driving, Chell made a few turns on more local roads and the scenery became much more rural. Large fields surrounded them, broken up by the occasional rundown barn or house.

"This place went dead well before the Crisis came. No one had a use for small farms anymore. Not enough people wanted to buy fresh eggs from their local Farmer Bob anymore, so Farmer Bob and his clan either had to move out or starve to death," Chell continued as Axel surveyed the area.

"So why would the Sanctuary be here?" he asked, still facing the window.

"You know what borders the city, right?"

"Yeah. The Atlantic."

"Precisely. The Atlantic Ocean. You know when the city was founded?"

"Some time in the mid-1500s, if I'm not mistaken."

"You're not. Mid-1500s. A New World port town fabled with exotic riches and Native women. I wonder what sort of crowd that would have attracted."

"Pirates. Smugglers. Outlaws."

"Precisely. And that sort of folk would need somewhere to store their goods, don't you think?"

Axel stared blankly as he tried to connect the pieces. "An underground hideout."

"Bingo."

Axel let out a small laugh of disbelief. "So, you're telling me that those hideouts we've been going to around the city…they're former smugglers' dens?"

"Ah, they were more than just dens, love," Chell replied seriously. "They were complex underground byways, complete with fortified tunnels that connect from all parts of the district. Many of the tunnels go right under the heart of the city."

"And no one knows about them? No unsuspecting archeologist or curious punk accidently stumbled upon one of these entrances?"

"If anyone did, they certainly aren't in any state to say anything. Even after the whole 'Age of Exploration' thing was over, the system was still used. Secret goods and arms shipments during the Revolution, information and medicine during the Civil War, bootleg liquor during the Prohibition Era. They weren't completely abandoned until after the Cold War. Those who knew about it died out; it became more myth than anything else. Luckily for us, an early Ordumbra member dug up some old records and 'rediscovered' them. The Order has been using them ever since."

Chell then went off the road onto a dusty path. It cut through an abandoned field filled with dead grass. As they drove, a large, brick factory building came into view.

"That's the Sanctuary?" Axel asked doubtfully.

"It's only the entrance. Trust me, it gets better. Much better," Chell replied in earnest.

She kept driving towards the building until a dirt path became visible. She then started to slow as they neared a tall gate made of ebony steel. Guard booths flanked either side of them but no one was in them. Other than the pair in the car, there seemed to be no other sources of human life.

Chell stopped in front of the metal barricade. The partners then stepped out of the car and walked over to one of the booths. An eerie silence surrounded them as they stood in front of the door. Chell stepped forward and held her hand up. Suddenly, a bright blue laser shot out from the top of the doorway and scanned her entire body. Then, as quickly as it came out, the laser disappeared; on the wall, a hidden screen displayed Chell's name and credentials. Axel walked forward as Chell moved away and the process repeated itself. Once the screen turned black after showing Axel's information, two blue lights shot out from both guard booths and passed over Chell's car. When they finished, a buzzer sounded and the gates slowly retracted.

Axel jogged over to the passenger's side as Chell slipped back into the driver's seat. She drove to the side of the building and turned the engine off. Chell grabbed her bag from the backseat, left the keys in the ignition, and exited the car with Axel. They hurried to the entrance of the decrepit building. Inside was a monstrous but nearly empty room. The floor was earthen and not a single piece of furniture or machinery remained. From the walls, however, hung bright flags of crimson and coal that bore the Ordumbra crest. Straggling rays of sunlight streamed in and illuminated small patches of the vacant space. Chell and Axel went to a dull olive door hidden in the shadows. A retinal scanner was mounted on the wall. Axel went and bent down in front of it; another blue beam shot out and swept over his eye. The scanner let out a small beep and the door slip open. The pair went through and entered a small but brighter room. A modern glass elevator was the room's sole feature. Chell strode forward and pressed a button. The doors opened automatically and the two stepped in. She pressed another button and the elevator quietly descended deep under the main factory. When they reached their destination and the doors opened, they stepped out and were met by two masked and armored figures wielding automatic rifles. The guards nodded to the pair before opening the metal door they were keeping watch over. Chell went forward with Axel close behind her.

Past the door was a low but wide tunnel with small light bulbs running along the ceiling. Though clean and illuminated with electrical lights, much of the tunnel was left alone. The ecru stone walls still had their original mortar; symbols and messages graced the walls, revealing a rich but complicated history. The two walked briskly to get to the end. As they passed, smaller tunnels from the other hideouts opened into the main one, the names of each respective region painted above the archways. They continued on until they reached a room much taller than the tunnel. On the other side was the door to the underground headquarters: an enormous steel masterpiece covered in arabesque carvings with the Ordumbra crest in the center. To the side of it was a long, tasseled pulley. Chell wrapped her fingers around the golden mass and pulled on it hard. Inside, the sound of bells could be distinctly heard. Axel and Chell stood back while someone on the other end unlocked the door. Axel raised an amused eyebrow at the sound of multiple bolts sliding open.

"Huh. They certainly seemed prepared," he replied as the clicking continued.

"This area is ready for anything. There are tons of guards outside, hidden in the shadows, always ready to strike. If hostiles approach, they alert the two guards we just passed and try to hold them off. Those two will run down here and start the attack system." She turned and motioned down the hallway. "Eight steel doors close all down this hallway and others close off the smaller tunnels. Don't let the old-looking walls fool you; they're all rigged with motion detectors and machine guns. Anyone who even thinks about breaking in here will be slaughtered on the spot."

"And if they do manage to kill all the guards outside and get to this door?" Axel asked, bending his head back to look at the monstrous doorway.

"The time that it would take to get here would give everyone enough time to escape through a series of hidden tunnels and passageways. We'd all go out towards the sea. Then, the entire headquarter would detonate. No evidence left behind."

"Impressive," Axel said with a smile as the door majestically opened. They walked into a small, dimly-lit room and were greeted by a tall, pale fellow draped in a black coat.

"This way, mister and miss," he said, beckoning the two to follow him. On the far wall, there was another steel door, but not as fancy. It had a wheel instead of a knob, similar to doors found on old submarines.

"Before I let you in, I must scan you. Please stand still," the man said as he grabbed a black security wand from a hook. He passed it over both Axel and Chell before grunting in approval. Then, the man put his hands firmly on the wheel and turned it clockwise, creating grinding metallic sounds. Finally, the man pulled the door open and bowed before the two.

"Farewell. Make us a new world," the doorman said as he held the door open. The couple gave appreciative nods before going inside. Axel looked up and inhaled deeply upon seeing the headquarters' antechamber.

Tall, white columns rose up from the marble floor and fanned out into Gothic arches high above them. Golden medallions studded the ceiling and reflected the soft candlelight from dozens of hanging brass candelabras. Little alcoves around the hall housed posh small, claw-footed tables surrounded by posh Louis XIV chairs. Oriental vanities lined the walls with great bouquets of exotic flowers resting on top. Giant landscapes in ornate frames hung against the wall underneath a line of Ordumbra flags. Chell led Axel down the long, cochineal carpet that ran across the hall. At the end was a large fountain in the shape of a woman. She held aloft a mighty sword while bearing a glass orb in her other hand. A human skull rested at her feet with a large, gilded bird sitting on top: a phoenix. Water poured out from the orb and the phoenix's open beak while an amulet bearing the fiery insignia of the Order gleamed on the woman's chest.

"It's this way. We need to get to the draft room. Not as splendid, but certainly worth seeing," said Chell, tugging Axel away from the statue. They went around it up a flight of marble steps and proceeded down another long hallway. The landscapes on the walls turned to portraits of past Masters of the Order of Shadows. Their dark hoods signifying rank shrouded their eyes, but they seemed to watch the couple go down the hallway. Chell led Axel down a small flight of stairs that led to yet another doorway.

Inside was a massive, ovular room filled with all types of people and technology. It split into two levels, each with its own distinct function. On the upper level, where Chell and Axel were standing, was the think tank. Rows of sophisticated computers filled the space along with an amalgamation of printers, telephones, and fax machines. Off to the right were dozens of tall file cabinets filled with years of research and Ordumbra visions. People of all races weaved through the desks carrying papers, file folders, and cups of coffee. Small groups huddled together and the summation of their quiet chatter formed an excited buzz; the final preparation had begun. Guards in black muscle shirts and fatigue pants mulled around the area, but were clearly as excited as the researchers. In one corner, there were two fully armed guards standing outside of a solid-looking metal door. Chell's heart raced as she remembered where the door led to; there was a large underground garage for the killing machines.

Chell pointed to the lower level. "That's where we're supposed to go," she said to Axel. The lower level was a large theatre like filled with forty cushioned benches. In the front was a great mahogany podium elevated about two feet from the ground. Many people were already at this level and began to situate themselves. Chell latched onto Axel's muscled arm as he escorted her down the elegantly carpeted staircase. When they reached the bottom, Chell was greeted by a tide of familiar faces; most congratulated her on the destruction of Coronus. After justly receiving her compliments, she and Axel settled onto a bench off to the side.

For ten minutes they waited, squeezing each other's hands in excitement. Then, a loud hum came from behind. Chell turned around to see thick floor-to-ceiling dividers emerge from the walls, separating the lower and upper level. When the two doors finally shut, no sound could be heard from the boisterous office space behind. The congregation then turned their eyes to the podium, which was no longer devoid of a speaker. In front was a tall but aged figure cloaked in robes of pitch black and gold. His hood concealed his eyes with an impenetrable shadow. Everyone in the room immediately stood up together. "Long live the Order! Long live the Order! Long live the Order!" they chanted together with great enthusiasm. It continued until the cloaked figure held up a hand. The chanting stopped and everyone took their seats.

"Welcome! Welcome!" the man's booming voice rang out as he swept his arms towards the crowd. "Indeed, ladies and gentlemen, this is a momentous day; so much has been accomplished, but so much still needs to be done. And now, the glorious rebirth shall begin! But first, let us reflect on what has been done today. The cities of Coronus and Peterstown were decimated today by our bomber squadrons. These cities housed rabid, ignorant people, filled with all sorts of corrupt ideology and immoral thoughts. But thanks to Commander Chelsea Greene, those philistines will no longer stand in our way."

There was tumultuous applause from all around as the operation leader stood. Chell bowed deeply before sitting back down. Axel leaned over and tipped her chin towards him before kissing her gently on her sweet lips. She blushed and drew closer to him.

"Yes. Applause well deserved for deeds well done. But today, friends, more needs to be accomplished. Today, the great machines engineered by our greatest minds will finally be put out into the streets, and all of you, as leading commanders, shall run them. You shall go forth and purge the land. We will finally begin the building of our new world! We will model it after the great phoenix of legend; from the ashes, greatness is reborn. By the powers of the Ordumbra, humankind shall be reborn!" the Master cried out, working himself into a state of frenzied fanaticism. Everyone in the auditorium burst into cheers. Axel and Chell were both amazed by the liveliness of the members around them; they were cheering, shouting, applauding, and even crying. A sense of grandeur blossomed in the hearts of the two. They were a part of this great and noble cause, one that would shape mankind for the rest of its existence.

Once again, the Master raised his hand. The commanders fell silent at once, waiting attentively for the next statement.

"In this city, corrupt leaders command the people, leading them around like marionettes. They breed fear and hate among the populace, rendering them irrational and unstable. That ends today. This city is to be utterly destroyed. Bring down the buildings of these hypocrites and charlatans. Have no fear of whom you kill.

Those who remain in those crumbling homes are not Order members; they are villains set against us. Kill all who try to flee or resist."

The Master pressed a small button on the podium and a diagram of the necrotanks appeared on a projector screen. He turned towards the image.

"Now, for the tanks themselves. They are equipped with five Miniguns, two on each side of the tank and one in the back. In the front, the self-loading warhead launcher. There will be two commanders per unit. You will have five gunmen in the lower decks of the Necrotanks who have all been instructed to fire at will. Solid steel and titanium armor. Able to crush anything in its path. The tank is indestructible. Truly, the pinnacle of Ordumbra engineering and design," the hooded man indicated as he pointed out each detail.

Spreading his arms again, he continued with an air of fatherly pride. "My children, it is time. Similar operations are taking place overseas as we speak. It is time for you to go out into the world and smite those who threaten the human race. We will forever change the face of history. Now go. There is no room for error. Only victory. Set forth and bring about the renewal of the human race! Go and fulfill the divine prophecy!"

The room burst into an uproar as the Master stepped off of the podium. The people in the auditorium rushed to his side, wanting to shake hands or to thank or simply touch the man. The dividers slowly separated and the upper level became visible. One by one, the commanders went up the steps and filed towards the guarded metal door. Chell and Axel stood, but Chell put her hand on his arm.

"Wait for me. I'll be back shortly," she whispered before planting a kiss on his cheek. She ran towards a guarded door, slid her ID card, and entered. The area looked like the inside of a hotel. She went down the wide hallway, reading the room numbers as she did. Finally, she arrived to room 523 and knocked. The door opened and Chell's mother stood in the doorway.

"Chell! Honey, what's happening?" she cried as she threw her arms around her daughter. From behind, she could see her grandmother. They had visitors: Axel's parents.

"It's time, Mom. We're going now," Chell said softly.

Chell's mother said nothing, but gazed into her daughter's eyes. She then placed her hands on the sides of Chell's head and kissed her forehead.

"Go and do what you need to do, sweetheart," she whispered as tears flooded her eyes.

Chell hugged her mother again, then went inside the room. She kissed her grandmother and shook hands with Axel's parents.

"I'll keep him out of trouble. Don't you worry," Chell said with a sad smile. Axel's father nodded with a grimace while his wife began to cry. Chell then walked out of the room, waved through the doorway, and left.

By the time she met back up with Axel, the last few commanders were leaving. She glided next to him and put a hand on his arm.

"I'm ready," Chell said quietly.

"As am I."

They looked at each other, taking in the sparks of glee in each other's eyes. Both were ready for what was to come.

****

"I'm driving," Axel yelled as they raced towards the Necrotank they were assigned to. The two stopped in front of the great weapon, marveling at the sheer power that the tank commanded; the power that they would soon be commanding. It was long and as tall as a double-decker bus. It looked nothing like the tanks they've seen in war movies. The entire thing looked like it was made of solid corpse-light; it was a sickly pale green that seemed to radiate death. Axel gripped the cold metal climbing handles on the side of the tank and pulled himself up. He scaled it and waited for Chell. Then, he unlocked the heavy cupola and slowly climbed down the ladder. He reached the bottom and stood back. Chell ignored the ladder and jumped down the hatch, landing in a crouched position on the floor. She straightened herself up and grinned at Axel, who rolled his eyes. They then looked around at the interior; it was equally as impressive as the outside. It was tight but superiorly high-tech. The wall was decked with switchboards and flashing lights. There were seats set for the gunmen, the missile-launcher, the driver, and the assistants.

"It's time, love," Chell said as they quickly kissed.

"Indeed. Today, we go to glory," Axel said, gripping her hand and squeezing it gently.

"Right. I'll be in contact," she said nodding. Then, she walked over to the seat and adjusted it. She felt all of her training flooding back to her as she flipped the numerous switches overhead. Chell grabbed the headset on the side and fitted it over her head.

"Testing, testing. Station one checking in," she said into the microphone.

"Station two checking in," Axel said from below.

"Station three checking in."

"Station four checking in."

The rest of the group checked in and finished their pre-departure proceedings.

"Is the artillery ready to go?" a gunman asked.

"Yes. Everything's ready. All we're waiting for now is the go-ahead from the Master."

Chell and Axel, who had views from the front of the tank, watched the Master and the flagman converse with each other. There was a moment where nothing happened, but then the hooded man nodded at the flagman with a smile on his face. Then, he turned to some unseen person and raised his hand. Up above, great doors opened up. The overcast sky gave off an ominous, joyless light. The floor gave a strong lurch and started rising upwards towards the dead sky. Chell watched in amazement as the twenty necrotanks and their leaders ascended to ground level. After a few moments, they reached outside and the movement stopped with a grinding halt. Up above, they were closer to the city than where they entered. A long paved road led from the barren encampment out to an empty back road; this was how they would be entering the city.

The Master put his wrist close to his lips and spoke into the microphone. Inside, the crewmembers of the necrotanks heard his transmission.

"My friends, it is time. Go with courage. Go with strength. Go and build the new world!" he said with pride. The flagman next to him gave the signal for them to proceed out.

"Let's go," Axel said as he shifted the tank into gear and slowly crept into line with the others. The high, concertina wire-topped gates that surrounded the area were pushed opened by workers.

"Remember the formation. We're section C, so we go straight into the city. Don't touch the opening areas; open fire solely in the city," Chell reminded them. "We're going straight for the Society building. I want to see that thing burned to the ground. "

"Aye aye, Captain. One decimated building coming up," the third gunman replied with a grin.

They slowly made their way along with the rest of the tanks. They pushed through the narrow roads, crushing garbage cans and newspaper stands. Few people were on these streets; the few that were watched the tanks with horrified wonder. The one-way road diverged into smaller ones and the cluster of tanks began to disband and go in separate directions. They separated in groups; five going left, five going right, and ten going straight. The heavier firepower would be necessary for the densely-populated center of the city. This was where Chell was going.

"I see skyscrapers!" Axel sang as the tall buildings became visible. More people could be seen now, many of whom were peering at the Necrotanks in a mix of fear and curiosity.

"Open artillery doors," Chell ordered.

"Opening doors, commander."

The Miniguns were exposed on all of the tanks. Chell and her company pulled ahead into the heart of the city and positioned themselves at an angle across the street from the Society building.

"Get ready, boys," Chell said to her crew. She then spoke into her headset. "T-13, T-14, T-15, do you all read me?"

"We read you, T-12," came the reply. Another tank pulled ahead and aimed itself at the building. On the other side of the building, two more tanks were doing the same.

"All ready?" a voice asked on the headset. Chell's heart raced in her chest; she could feel the adrenaline pumping through her. "Ready," she answered.

"Then go."

"OPEN FIRE!" Chell yelled to the rest of her company.

A shot rang out as the tank fired at the base of the building. It exploded on contact, blowing up cars and charring the surrounding area. The glass lobby shattered and the interior was engulfed in flames. Through the smoke, a few desperate people tried crawling out of the building. The other tanks began firing as well, killing all who tried to escape. Chell aimed to where she thought the elevators were and fired. Sure enough, she hit her mark. The warhead sent a column of fire up into the elevator shafts, disabling them. The building was besieged from all sides, spreading fire to the surrounding buildings. Chell readjusted her trajectory and aimed higher. She launched a missile into a cluster of fifth-story offices. The shot penetrated the glass but collided into a central beam. The floor was obliterated on contact, sending bursts of fire and shards of glass in all directions.

Meanwhile, citizens tried to escape. They ran, screaming in terror with their arms over their heads. Children clung to mothers, wives to husbands; no amount of defending would save them from the Order. The gunmen opened fire, shooting down all in their path. The people dropped like birds shot in midflight. Their bodies littered the ground as blood pooled around them. Chell continued her battle against the Society building and everyone inside. It was badly burned, with multiple floors completely consumed in flames. Twisted metal was scattered on the ground next to the burning shells of blown-out cars. Inside the tank, the crew could not hear the sickening smack of flesh hitting pavement; desperate workers from the higher floors had exited the building the hard way, deciding to immediately smite themselves rather than endure the pain slowly and torturously.

"There's more that has to be done. All units, move back," Chell told her team as well as the others. As Axel repositioned them farther away, she held up a small square remote with a black button under a small door. She took a key that hung on a chain around her neck and unlocked the door. She held her hand over the button while watching the building. Then, she slammed her hand down. From the building came a tremendous explosion. It ripped through the base like a frenzied animal. Fire and smoke rippled up the battle-weary building and formed a mushroom cloud around the middle. The sounds of grinding metal and breaking glass penetrated the barriers of the tank as the structure began to succumb to its wounds. Chell and Axel watched as the entire building began to lean and sway. The impetus of the building triumphed and the left side of the building noisily gave way; the entire building came crashing down on its side like a giant oak tree. It appeared to be falling in slow motion as the leviathan structure bore down on the neighboring buildings in a fiery cloud of glass, metal, and flesh. The smaller offices next to the Society headquarters were crushed like bugs under the weight. They sagged for a few seconds before collapsing in on themselves, sending the Society building completely to the ground. The small office building let out a large explosion, relighting the defeated headquarters. Fires raged across the lots and boiling water shot up from the broken pipes under the facilities. Bodies of the men and women who didn't escape lay charred and bloodied; those that were visible were viciously mangled and nearly unidentifiable. The screams and prayers of the dying feebly floated up from the ruins.

Chell let out an excited yell. The place she hated the most, the stem of all of her problems, was finally destroyed. As the gunmen busied themselves with the fleeing, Axel spoke up.

"Guys, we've got resistance coming this way. The police are finally here," he announced loudly to the team, watching the incoming armored cars.

"What the hell took 'em so long? I was gettin' bored!" one gunman yelled over the deafening roar of the guns.

Chell pulled her headset closer and addressed the rest of the tank commanders. "We've got incoming police forces. We'll need assistance to fully clear them."

"Roger. We've got your back," came the reply. The Necrotanks turned away from the burning rubble and assumed a v-formation. There were scores of armored police cars lined up, as well as those from the SWAT Team. They formed a barricade as officers rushed forward with riot shields, guns, and RPGs. Chell could see the fear in their eyes; they knew that they were going to be dead in a matter of minutes. A malicious smile played upon her face as she realized the power she possessed; she, along with Axel and the others, controlled whether men and women lived or died. Surely, she thought, there was no greater power than that.

"Hold positions, everyone!" she bellowed into the headset. The gunmen ceased fire on the civilians and waited for the battle to fully ensue.

The girl aimed carefully at a cluster of police officers. At that moment, she knew. The beginning of the end was near for the world, and from it would rise again a new and glorious nation. One that she had shaped with the blood of her loved ones and the might of her own soul. The Society would continue to pay for what they had done, but now her personal vendetta was intertwined with the goals of the Order. Chell recalled her dream and the options given to her by the sorceress; turn back or see the light. She laughed at the irony. She saw the tank as the arm to grasp the door handle; what lay beyond the door, she knew not. But it mattered little; for it was too late to turn back.

Then, it happened.

Spontaneously, an eerie blue light consumed the girl's hand. It sent sparks up her arm that empowered her body and her mind. She could feel the light's unearthly energy surging through every fiber of her being. At once, Chell knew what was happening. Finally, the destiny assigned to her in the fateful dream had fulfilled itself: she now wielded true power. She threw her head back and laughed triumphantly. Those in the tank watched in amazement. One by one, they began to laugh, too.

Suddenly, sparks of sharp pain shot up Chell's arm as she let out a small scream. The rest of the team stared at her, just as confused as she was. The pain intensified as the light shifted to a crimson red. Something was wrong. Something was terribly wrong. Chell could feel it but could not understand. Axel screamed her name and ran towards the ladder. Time halted as consciousness slowly slipped out of Chell's grasp. The sounds of Axel's shouting and the screams from outside magnified in her mind as darkness overtook her.

OMEN

The sky slowly colored carnelian as the sun sunk down into the desert's edge. A sharp, arid wind whipped through the area, sending a vortex of sand across the surface. A horned lizard scurried up the side of a dune and looked westward. Below it was a lonely, winding road that led to a massive, slate-gray biomedical facility. No movement came from the building except for a white smoke cloud that rose lazily from a smokestack and a handful of guards patrolling around the entrance.

Deep under the main compound, two men in pristine hazmat suits operated in a cold laboratory. One peered through a thick, glass container which housed a fat, clearly-infected mouse. He picked a container up from the rack and brought it to his workstation before switching on an overhead floodlight. His identification tag, bearing the name 'Jacob Williams', reflected the light in all directions.

"Oh my god. Adam, you have to see this!" Jacob exclaimed to his partner as he opened up the container and held the sick rodent in his hand.

"Just tell me what you see. I'm busy," Adam replied dryly. He held down a healthy mouse and slowly injected it with a dark red serum: blood tainted with the Endellia virus, a Category 4 biohazard.

"This virus! It's absolutely incredible! Cold sweats, blood-filled pustules, profound disorientation, possible internal hemorrhaging...and this mouse was injected a week ago! Usually, it takes three weeks to get to this point. This is one hell of a strain!"

Jacob exclaimed through his headset. "I need to see what this thing's blood cells are like."

Adam rolled his eyes and put his mouse back into its container. He looked up at the black cameras in the room and winked. He knew they couldn't see anything; he had paid handsomely for the cameras to go blind. Quickly, he took two vials of contaminated blood from a rack and replaced them with vials filled with a similar liquid. He then carefully wrapped the real tubes in suede cloth before taping them inconspicuously to the wrist of his suit. He stole multiple glances at his partner, but Jacob kept his back turned. Adam then walked over to the door.

"I'll be back. Gotta run to the loo," he announced as he punched in numbers into a keypad. A buzzer rang and the door slid open with a whoosh. He walked into the cleansing chamber and was shrouded in a sheer disinfecting mist. He then took off the constricting suit and peeled the taped parcel from it. Adam walked into the outer chamber where his jacket hung on a hook and slipped the two vials into the pocket. After going to the bathroom, he returned and suited back up. He nonchalantly walked in and went back to the station.

"You ever think about what would happen if this ever got out? Like, if Endellia ever spread?" Jacob asked as he primed another mouse to be injected.

"Of course not. It's too horrible of a thought. You've seen what it does to mice. God knows what it'll do to us." Adam turned back to his station, but brooded over Jacob's statement. He had indeed thought about what the virus would do to human subjects. The blood, the insanity, the fever dreams. The very thought of the sickness and the wanton destruction that would ensue made him delightfully giddy.

A sharp yell interrupted his fantasies. Jacob rushed out of the lab and into the disinfecting unit. He violently stripped off the wrappings on his gloves and peeled the layers away as the cleansing mist enveloped him.

"Jake, Jake! What the hell happened? Did you stab yourself?" Adam asked through his headset, trying to get a clear look at him from inside the lab.

"Yeah. I got distracted when I was injecting the mouse and...I don't know, the damn thing slipped," Jacob replied frantically as he took off the final layer. He examined his finger and his face paled as Adam asked, "Did it break the skin?"

"No. I'm...I'm alright," he lied as he saw a bead of blood emerge from the wound. He quickly wiped it off and replaced his compromised gloves with fresh ones. Soon after, he rejoined his co-worker, trying to steady his breath.

"You seem sorta shaken up there, Jake. You sure you're ok?" Adam asked, an edge of slyness creeping into his voice.

"Yeah, yeah. I'm fine, man," Jacob replied. He turned away from Adam so he wouldn't see the tears welling up in his eyes. It didn't matter, though; Adam already knew the truth.

Damn, Adam thought to himself as he watched Jacob closely, *there was supposed to be only one Patient Zero. This one has to go.*

He looked at the clock on the wall. It was seven in the evening: time for the day shift to leave and for the night shift to begin.

"Time to leave, man. Time for me to get roaring drunk on this fine Friday night," he said as he put away the test tube racks and dropped the used needles in the biohazard collection bin. He walked over to his colleague, who had not said a word since the accident, and clapped him on the shoulder.

"Why don't you come with me? It'll be fun!" Adam asked. When Jacob hesitated, he gave him a playful punch on the arm. "Come on, it'll be fine. Hit up a couple of bars, pick up girls, we'll have a good time! No point in you spending such a great night alone. Besides, you need to lighten up; the needle didn't go through. You haven't started baying at the moon or anything yet, so stop worrying! What do you say?"

Jacob smiled. "Alright, fine," he replied, turning off the laboratory lights. He and Adam got disinfected and changed out of their suits before putting on their jackets. Other virologists followed behind Adam and Jacob as they made their way across the industrial metal walkway that led to the circular elevator. The steps of the departing echoed through the vast underground annex. As they waited for the elevator doors to open, Adam's friend Jim came up behind him.

"Evening, Adam, Jake. How'd your day go?" he asked the pair as the doors opened and everyone stepped inside?

"Fairly run of the mill. I'm getting sick of seeing half-dead mice, to be honest," Adam replied while Jacob watched the floors go by.

"So no cure, huh?" Jim inquired, turning towards Adam.

"Nope. We haven't found anything," Adam answered, but he made direct eye contact with his friend and looked quickly downwards before looking up and meeting Jim's gaze. Jim nodded slightly and turned away.

"Oh, well. We'll get there eventually," he said, then remained quiet.

Adam subtly moved his hand over to his right hip. There, wrapped in a silk handkerchief, was another small vial he had stolen earlier: a vial filled with the clear antidote for the Endellia virus.

Adam smiled. He had both the poison and its cure. The Master would certainly be pleased.

www.ingramcontent.com/pod-product-compliance
Lightning Source LLC
Chambersburg PA
CBHW020250150626
46552CB00020B/756